"Are the *kinder* ⎯

Uncomfortable with his ⎯
family, Carolyn said, "Kevin had a bad dream and woke us up."

"Because of the rain?"

"It's possible."

"Rebuilding a building is easy. Rebuilding one's sense of security isn't."

"That sounds like the voice of experience."

Michael sighed. "My parents died when I was young, and both my twin brother and I had to learn not to expect something horrible was going to happen without warning."

"I'm sorry. I should have asked more about you and the other volunteers. I've been wrapped up in my own tragedy."

"At times like this, nobody expects you to be thinking of anything but getting a roof over your *kinder*'s heads."

He didn't reach out to touch her, but she was aware of every inch of him so close to her. His quiet strength had awed her from the beginning. As she'd come to know him better, his fundamental decency had impressed her more. He was a man she believed she could trust.

She shoved that thought aside. Trusting any man would be the worst thing she could do.

Jo Ann Brown has always loved stories with happily-ever-after endings. A former military officer, she is thrilled to have the chance to write stories about people falling in love. She is also a photographer and travels with her husband of more than thirty years to places where she can snap pictures. They have three children and live in Florida. Drop her a note at joannbrownbooks.com.

Books by Jo Ann Brown

Love Inspired

Green Mountain Blessings

An Amish Christmas Promise

Amish Spinster Club

The Amish Suitor
The Amish Christmas Cowboy
The Amish Bachelor's Baby
The Amish Widower's Twins

Amish Hearts

Amish Homecoming
An Amish Match
His Amish Sweetheart
An Amish Reunion
A Ready-Made Amish Family
An Amish Proposal
An Amish Arrangement

Visit the Author Profile page at Harlequin.com for more titles.

An Amish
Christmas Promise

Jo Ann Brown

 HARLEQUIN® LOVE INSPIRED®

Recycling programs
for this product may
not exist in your area.

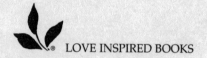

LOVE INSPIRED BOOKS

ISBN-13: 978-1-335-47955-6

An Amish Christmas Promise

Copyright © 2019 by Jo Ann Ferguson

www.Harlequin.com

Printed in U.S.A.

Bear ye one another's burdens,
and so fulfil the law of Christ.
For if a man think himself to be something,
when he is nothing, he deceiveth himself.
But let every man prove his own work,
and then shall he have rejoicing in himself
alone, and not in another.
For every man shall bear his own burden.
—*Galatians* 6:2–5

For Amanda,
who keeps us looking good

Chapter One

Evergreen Corners, Vermont

The bus slowed with a rumble of its diesel engine.

Michael Miller opened his eyes. A crick in his neck warned him that he'd fallen asleep in a weird position. The last time he'd ridden a bus was when he caught one to the train station in Lancaster, Pennsylvania. Then he'd traveled with his twin brother and Gabriel's *bopplin* to their new farm in Harmony Creek Hollow in northern New York.

Now he was on a bus on a late October day because he needed time away, time with peace and quiet, to figure out the answer to one vital question: Should he remain in their Amish community, or was the future he wanted beyond a plain life?

Today Michael was in Vermont, on his way to Evergreen Corners. The small village was at the epicenter of powerful flash floods that had accompanied Hurricane Kevin when the massive storm stalled over the eastern slopes of the Green Mountains last week.

The bus hit another pothole in the dirt on what once

had been a paved road. He was shocked to discover the other lane had been washed away. The road, a major north–south conduit in the state, was barely wider than the bus's wheels. He didn't see any cars anywhere, just a couple of trucks with what looked like a town seal on their doors. They were parked near a building where all the windows and doors were missing.

His stomach tightened. Had those vehicles been commandeered as ambulances? Were the people working there looking for victims?

The stories coming out of Vermont had warned that the situation was dismal. Whole sections of towns like Evergreen Corners had been washed away by torrents surging along what had been babbling brooks. People left with no place to live, all their possessions gone or covered with thick mud. Trees torn from the banks. Rocks—both giant boulders and tons of gravel—swept beneath bridges and damming the streams, forcing the water even higher.

Michael could see the road—or what there was left of it—followed a twisting stream between two steep mountains. The job of rebuilding was going to be bigger than he'd imagined when he'd stepped forward to offer his skills as a carpenter.

How much could he and the other fifteen volunteers on the bus do in the next three months? Where did they begin?

And what had made him think he'd find a chance to think about the future *here*?

God, I trust You know where I should be. Help me see.

The bus jerked to a stop, and the driver opened the door. "Here we are!"

A pungent odor oozed into the bus. It was a disgusting mix of mud and gasoline and the fuel oil that had been washed out of household storage tanks. Michael gasped, choking on the reek.

When a mask was held out to him, he took it from his friend, Benjamin Kuhns, who was sitting beside him, but didn't put it on. Like Michael, Benjamin had volunteered when a representative of Amish Helping Hands had come two days ago to Harmony Creek Hollow. Amish Helping Hands worked with other plain organizations to help after natural disasters. Benjamin announcing that he wanted to come, too, had been a surprise, because he'd been focused for the past year on working with his older brother, Menno, in getting their sawmill running. Business had been growing well, and Michael wondered if Benjamin was seeking something to help him grasp onto his future, too.

"Watch where you step," shouted the bus driver before he went out.

Michael stood and grabbed his small bag off the shelf over his head, stuffing the mask into a pocket. He noticed a few people on the bus had donned theirs.

His larger bag, where he'd packed the tools he expected he'd need, was stored under the bus. Nobody spoke as they filed out, and he knew he wasn't the only person overwhelmed by the destruction.

As his feet touched the muddy ground, he heard, "Look out!"

He wasn't sure whether to duck, jump aside or climb back on the bus. Looking around, he saw a slender blonde barreling toward him, arms outstretched.

Squawking was the only warning he got before a small brown chicken ran into him, bounced backward, turned and kept weaving through the crowd of volunteers moving to get their luggage from beneath the bus. The chicken let out another terrified screech before vanishing through a forest of legs and duffels.

The woman halted before she ran into him, too. Putting out her hands, she stopped two *kinder* from colliding with him. The force of their forward motion drove her a step closer, and he dropped his bag to the ground and caught her by the shoulders before she tumbled over the toes of his weather-beaten work boots. He was astounded that though her dress was a plain style, the fabric was a bright pink-and-green plaid.

"Are you okay?" Michael asked.

She nodded and looked at him with earth-brown eyes that seemed the perfect complement to her pale hair. She was so short her head hardly reached his shoulder. Her features were delicate. Thanking him, she turned to the *kinder.*

He hadn't expected the simple act of gazing into her pretty eyes to hit him like the recoil of a mishandled nail gun. Was she plain, or dressed simply because she was cleaning up the mess left by the flood?

He glanced at the *kinder* who'd been chasing her and the chicken. The boy appeared to be around six or seven years old. He had light brown hair, freckles and blue-gray eyes. Along with jeans and sneakers, he wore a T-shirt stained with what looked like peanut butter and jelly. Beside him, and wearing almost identical clothing, though without the stains, the little girl had hair the same soft honey-blond as the woman's. Like the boy, she had freckles, but her eyes were dark. When she grinned at him, she revealed she'd lost her two front teeth.

He couldn't keep from smiling. The *kind* was adorable, and he could imagine how she'd be twisting boys' hearts around her finger in a few years.

Just as Adah Burcky had with every guy who'd glanced her way. What a *dummkopf* he'd been to think he was the sole recipient of her kisses and flirtatious glances! He could hear her laugh when she'd walked away with another man. There had been a hint of triumph in it, as if she took delight in keeping track of the hearts she broke…including his.

What had brought Adah to mind? He'd come to Evergreen Corners to decide what he wanted to do with his future, not to focus on the past. For too long, he'd been drifting, following his twin brother to their new home, a place where he wasn't sure he belonged. Was his life among the plain folk, or was the route God had mapped for him meant to take him somewhere else? He had three months to figure that out.

"She's getting away," the boy insisted in an ever-louder voice, breaking into Michael's thoughts. "We've got to catch her before she gets hit by a car."

"There aren't a lot of cars on the road," the woman replied, ruffling his hair in an attempt to calm him.

"But there are buses." The boy flung out a hand toward the one that had brought Michael to Evergreen Corners. "See?"

Michael wasn't the only one trying to stifle a grin as the woman said, "We'll pray she'll be fine, Kevin. Place her in God's hands and trust He knows what's best."

Though he thought the boy would protest, the *kind* nodded. "Like you placed us in God's hands when the brook rose."

She nodded, but her serene facade splintered for a second. By the time she'd turned to Michael, it was again in place, and he wondered if he'd imagined the shadows in her eyes.

"I'm so sorry," she said. "We've been chasing Henrietta for the past fifteen minutes." She gave him a wry smile. "Not an original name for a chicken, but the kids chose our flock's names."

"She went that way." He pointed down the hill where a shallow brook rippled in the late-afternoon sunshine.

"She's headed toward our place, so maybe she'll turn up in what's left of our yard if she gets hungry enough." She wiped her forearm against her forehead and readjusted the black kerchief she wore over her honey-blond hair that was, he noticed for the first time, pulled into a tight bun at her nape.

"So your house is okay?" Michael asked.

She bit her lip before standing straighter. "No. Our house is gone."

He was shocked that anyone who'd lost their home could smile as she had. Could he have faced the situation with such aplomb and the *gut* spirits she did? That was a question he hoped he'd never have to answer.

Carolyn Wiebe knew she'd astounded the handsome dark-haired man who'd stepped off the bus. What had he expected her to do? Rage against the whims of nature? The storm that decimated everything she'd worked for during the past four years had been a mindless beast whose winds tore up the valley before sending water barreling down it. Be angry at God? How could she, when He'd spared their lives and everyone else's in Evergreen Corners? That hadn't been the situation in other towns, or so rumor whispered. No one could be sure of anything, but she'd heard of five deaths. People swept away as she and her children could have been. She'd made a promise to look after them forever, and she wasn't going to let a tempest change that.

Scanning the group from the bus, she dared to take a deep breath. She didn't see any sign of Leland Reber. There were other brown-haired men, but not the formerly plain man who'd married her late sister and had two youngsters with her. Though she hadn't seen his photo in over four years, she was sure she'd recognize him whether he dressed like her *Englisch* neighbors or in plain clothing. He had a square jaw with a cleft in his chin, which her sister Regina had found appealing...until the beatings started within weeks of their marriage.

For four years, Carolyn had managed to push Leland out of her mind while she focused on raising the children her sister had entrusted to her, children who called her Mommy. Then a neighbor had told her about hearing how Carolyn and the kids had been shown on national television news when reporters had appeared the day after the flood. If so, Leland, who'd embraced an *Englisch* life, most especially television and alcohol, could have learned where they were.

Carolyn's first thought had been to flee as they had when she'd left her beloved plain community in Indiana. She realized doing that was impossible when the roads were open only to authorized vehicles. Her car had been swept away in the flood and hadn't been found so she couldn't take Kevin and Rose Anne anywhere.

Her one consolation was Leland should have as much trouble getting to Evergreen Corners. The one way he could gain entry was to pretend to volunteer and get a ride with one of the disaster services. So she asked about vehicles bringing volunteers into Evergreen Corners, and she'd devised an excuse to be nearby when the newcomers had stepped off the bus. Today, Henrietta had provided her with one. She couldn't chance Leland sneaking into town and finding her and his son and daughter.

"Do you know where we're supposed to go, Mrs.—?" asked the man who'd been accosted by Henrietta.

He wasn't classically handsome. His straight nose was prominent, but his other features, especially his kind eyes, drew her attention away from it. Sharp cheekbones and a firm jaw suggested he wasn't someone to dismiss. In the sunlight that had shone every day after the hurricane, red accents glistened in the brown hair beneath his straw hat. The breadth of the black strap on his hat as well as his accent told her that he must be from Pennsylvania.

She warned herself to be cautious. Though Leland wasn't plain, he had many friends who were. Could he have sent one to look for her?

Stop being paranoid, she scolded herself. She wasn't worried for herself, but for her niece and nephew.

"I'm Carolyn Wiebe." She spoke the name without hesitation. She'd given it to herself after leaving Indiana, and she didn't correct his assumption she was married. Even in her thoughts, she sometimes forgot her real name was Cora Hilty. She was glad neither of the children recalled the surname they'd been given at birth. "This is Rose Anne, and that is Kevin."

"Kevin? Like Hurricane Kevin?"

"Appropriate for a five-year-old boy, don't you think?" She laughed at the surprise on the man's face. She didn't want to tell him that, with her emotions so raw, she had two choices: laugh or cry. During the day, she laughed. At night when everyone else was asleep, she gave in to tears at the thought of how the flood had taken her home and livelihood. With her kitchen gone, she could no longer bake pies and cookies for the diner in town as well as a trio of tourist farms not far out of town.

And laughing kept her from having to respond to the man's amazement when she said Kevin was five. She'd heard comments about how big he was for his age and how advanced he was. She'd brushed them aside, not wanting to admit the truth. Kevin was almost eighteen months older. She'd changed his age, as well as his sister's, to make it harder for Leland to locate these two sweet children. Assuming he was looking for them—and she had to—he would search for a nearly seven-year-old boy and a girl who'd had her fifth birthday. As far as the residents of Evergreen Corners knew, Rose Anne was four. More than one person had commented on how early she was losing her teeth, but that was always followed by a comment about how every kid was different.

"I'm Michael Miller," the man replied with a wink at Kevin. "They told us to report to a check-in center at the school. Can you point us in the right direction?"

"I'm heading that way. It's easier to show you than tell you." Her voice caught, but she rushed on, "Almost all the familiar landmarks are gone."

He nodded, and she saw his sympathy before he picked up the bag he'd dropped when she'd nearly run into him. His large duffel bag was set with others on a narrow patch of grass that had somehow not been washed away.

"We appreciate that, Mrs.—"

"Carolyn will do." She wasn't going to explain that her neighbors assumed she was a widow. Guilt tore at her each time she thought of the lies she had woven like a cocoon to protect Kevin and Rose Anne. "We're not big on formality."

After he'd introduced her to Benjamin Kuhns and

James Streicher, two men who'd traveled with him from an Amish settlement across the New York line, she motioned for the trio to follow her and the *kinder*.

Children! She needed to say "children" not *kinder*.

She must remember not to use *Deitsch*. Or act as if she understood it. She hadn't realized how much she'd missed hearing the Amish spoken language until these plain men began using it. But she had to seem as ignorant of it as her neighbors. Revealing she understood the language was one of the clues that, if repeated beyond the village, could draw Leland's attention to Evergreen Corners.

Holding Rose Anne's hand to stop the curious little girl from peering over the broken edge of the road, Carolyn made sure Kevin and the men were following her as she walked along the street toward the single intersection in the village. Nothing appeared as it had a week ago. Wide swaths of ground had been wiped clean by the rushing waters, and teetering buildings looked as if a faint breeze would send them crashing onto the sidewalks.

Michael moved to walk alongside her and Rose Anne as they passed ruined buildings. She heard Kevin regaling the other two men with tales of trying to recover their ten missing chickens.

"Do you think they survived?" Michael asked. "The chickens, I mean."

"We've seen most of them around the village. I opened the fence around the chicken coop before we evacuated." She pushed from her mind images of the horrifying moments when she and the children had struggled to escape the maddened waters.

She couldn't keep them from filling her nightmares, but she didn't intend to let those memories taint her waking hours. If they did, she might get distracted and fail to discover Leland had found them until it was too late. She couldn't take the chance he'd abduct Kevin and Rose Anne as he'd tried to before her sister died.

"And now everything is gone?" Michael asked, drawing her back from the abyss of her fears.

"Not everything."

"What's left?" he asked.

"Anything more than twenty-five feet above the brook survived, though several buildings were flooded a couple of feet into the first floor. The school, where we're headed, is the closest building to the brook that wasn't damaged at all."

He looked along the road running east and west through the village. "You're talking about more than five hundred feet away from the stream's banks."

"Uh-huh." She'd started to say *ja*, but halted herself. "Look at the mountains. They make this valley into a funnel, and the water kept rising and rising. We lost two restaurants and three shops as well as parts of the town hall, the fire station, the library, the elementary school, a building supply store. Also some historic buildings like the old gristmill that used to sit next to the brook. And, of course, a lot of houses, including a couple that had been here from when the town was founded in 1750. Many of the records were saved from the town hall, and, thankfully, the local newspaper had stored its back issues from the nineteenth century in the library, because their building washed away."

"What about the library books?" asked Benjamin. "Were the books saved?"

"A lot of them were lost. The cellar and first floor of the library were flooded, and many of the ones out on loan were washed away."

The men exchanged glances, but she looked at Kevin

and Rose Anne. She was glad they were talking to each other and paying no attention to the adults' conversation. Her arms ached as she remembered holding them and trying to comfort them after their escape from the flood. They'd been upset about losing their home, but having the library flooded had distressed them even more. They'd loved going there and borrowing books or listening to one read aloud to them.

"Though the books have gone swimming," Rose Anne, ever the diplomat, had said, as tears had welled in her eyes, "Jenna will tell us stories. She's nice, and she has lots and lots of the goriest stories."

Carolyn had translated Rose Anne's mangling of the language as she did each time Rose Anne came up with a new "version" of a word. She'd guessed the little girl meant *glorious* rather than *goriest*, but she hadn't wanted to take the time to ask. Instead, she'd offered the little girl what solace she could. However, after talking with her good friend Jenna Sommers, the village's librarian and the foster mother of a six-year-old little girl whom Rose Anne adored, Carolyn knew it would be many months— maybe even a year or two—before the library was operational again. First, people needed homes, and the roads had to be repaired and made safe.

And the children needed to be kept safe, too. Her sister had won full custody of the two children in the wake of her separation from Leland. He'd fought to keep them. Not because he wanted them. They would have been in the way of his rough life of drinking and drugs. He'd fought because he hadn't wanted his wife to have a single moment of joy. It hadn't been enough he'd left Regina with bruises and broken bones each time he bothered to come home. At last, her sister had agreed to let Carolyn help her escape the abuse. Regina had been free of her abusive husband for almost three months before she became ill and died two days later from what the *doktors* had said was a vicious strain of pneumonia.

"Wow," murmured one of the men behind her as they reached the main intersection where a concrete bridge's pilings were lost in a jungle of debris and branches. "Is there another bridge into town?"

"Not now. There was a covered bridge."

"Was it destroyed?" Michael asked.

"Half of it was except for a couple of deck boards. The other half's wobbly. From what I've heard, engineers will come next week to see what, if anything, can be salvaged."

"So the road we traveled in on the bus is the only way in or out?"

"For now." She didn't add it might be several months or longer before the lost and damaged bridges were repaired.

She led the men to higher ground. She listened as they spoke in hushed *Deitsch* about how difficult it would be to get supplies in for rebuilding. It was hard not to smile with relief while she listened to their practical suggestions. How splendid it was to have these down-to-earth men in Evergreen Corners! Instead of talking about paperwork and bureaucracy, they planned to get to work.

Hurrying up the street, Carolyn saw two of her chickens perched in a nearby tree. She was glad neither child noticed. Both were too busy asking the newcomers a barrage of questions.

The parking lot in front of the high school held news vans with their satellite dishes, so she cut across the lawn to avoid the curiosity of reporters looking for a few more stories before they headed to the next crisis. She nodded her thanks to Michael when he opened the door for her and the children but didn't slow while she strode along the hall that should have been filled with teenagers.

The temporary town hall was in the school's gym. She'd already heard grumbling from the students that the school had survived when so many other buildings hadn't. By the end of next week when school was scheduled to restart, she guessed most of them would be glad to be done with the drudgery of digging in the mud and get back to their books. Kevin and Rose Anne were growing more restless each day, and only the hunt for their chickens kept them from whining about it.

Voices reached out past the gym's open doors, and Carolyn said, "This is where volunteers are supposed to sign in. They'll get you a place to stay and your assignments." She flushed, realizing what she should have said from the beginning. "Thank you for coming to help us."

"More volunteers?" A man wearing a loosened tie and a cheerful smile came out of the gym, carrying a clipboard. Tony Whittaker was the mayor's husband. Asking their names, he pulled out a pen to check their names off. "Michael Miller, did you say?"

"Ja," Michael replied.

Tony's smile became more genuine. "I'm glad you and Carolyn have met already."

"Really?" she inquired at the same time Michael asked, "Why?"

"You, Michael, have been assigned to the team building Carolyn and her children a new home." He chuckled. "Hope you've made a good impression on each other, because you're going to be spending a lot of time together for the next three months."

Chapter Two

Carolyn woke to the cramped space in what once had been—and would again be—stables. The barn, along a ridge overlooking the village, was owned by Merritt Aiken, who had moved to Evergreen Corners after retiring from some fancy job in California.

The stables had become a temporary home for five families who'd been left homeless in the flood. Her cot, along with the two smaller ones the children used, left little room for any possessions in their cramped space in two stalls. They had only a few changes of clothing, donated by kind members of the Mennonite congregation.

Carolyn had been able to rescue Hopper, the toy rabbit Rose Anne had slept with since she was born. Somehow in the craziness of escaping the flood, she'd grabbed the wrong thing from Kevin's bed. Instead of his beloved Tippy, a battered dog who'd lost most of his stuffing years ago, she'd taken an afghan. Kevin had told her it was okay.

"I'm too big for a stuffed toy anyhow," he'd said.

She'd guessed he was trying to spare her feelings. That had been confirmed when the children were offered new stuffed toys. Kevin had thanked the volunteers and taken a bear, but it had been left on the floor by his cot. She'd caught sight of the stains of tears on his face after he'd fallen asleep and known he ached for his special toy.

It was too great a burden for a little boy to bear. The weight of everything they'd lost pressed down on her. It was difficult to act as if everything could be made right again. All she had from a week ago was the heart-shaped locket that had belonged to her sister and contained baby pictures of the children. It had taken her almost a month to get accustomed to wearing the necklace without feeling she was doing something wrong. A proper plain woman didn't wear jewelry, but she hoped God would understand she was fulfilling her sister's dying wish to keep the children close to her heart.

She clenched the gold locket as she savored the familiar scents of the barn. The dried hay and oats that had been a treat for the horses consigned to a meadow out back were a wonderful break from the odors closer to the brook. She let herself pretend she was a child again and had fallen asleep in her family's barn on a hot summer afternoon.

But she wasn't in that innocent time. She and the children were homeless, and she feared Leland would care enough about Kevin and Rose Anne to come to Vermont.

Assuming they'd been on the news, and he'd seen the report. Maybe he'd missed it.

Help me keep these children safe, she prayed.

The image of Michael Miller flashed through her mind, startling her. Why had she thought of him when she imagined being safe? It must be, she reassured herself, that he represented the Amish life she'd given up. Or maybe it was because he was going to be rebuilding their house. She shouldn't be envisioning his strong shoulders and easy smile, which had made her feel that everything was going to be okay simply because he was there.

She pushed herself up to sit. Was she out of her mind? Her sister and *mamm* had been enticed by good looks and charming talk, and both had suffered for it. Though *Daed* had never struck *Mamm*, at least as far as Carolyn knew, he'd berated her whenever something went wrong. Even if it'd been his fault. That abuse had continued until his death and had worn her mother down until she died the year before Carolyn left Indiana.

Carolyn heard the children shifting as they woke. She dressed and hushed Kevin as she helped him and his sister get ready for the day care center at the Mennonite meetinghouse's community center. The children had been going there while she helped prepare breakfast for the displaced and the volunteers.

After they'd made their beds and folded their night-clothes on top of the blankets, she held her finger to her lips as she led the way out of the barn.

Some of the people in the large barn were still asleep. With worries about when they'd have a home or a job to return to, many found it impossible to sleep through the night. She'd woken often during the long nights and heard people pacing or talking in anxious whispers. But, just as she did, the resilient Vermonters kept on their cheerful faces during the day.

Kissing the children and getting kisses in return, Carolyn watched as they joined the others at the low tables where they'd be served breakfast soon. She wasn't surprised Rose Anne chose a seat right next to Taylor, the librarian's foster daughter. Rose Anne and Taylor whispered in delight at seeing each other. Her niece had asked to have her hair done like Taylor's pom-pom pigtails, but Rose Anne's hair was too straight.

Carolyn waved to the women and one lone elderly man working at the day care center that morning.

Jenna Sommers, whose hair was as black as her foster daughter's, wove through the tables toward her, motioning for Carolyn to wait. More than one child halted the town's librarian and asked when she was going to read to them. Assuring them she would if they ate their breakfast, she was smiling as she reached the door where Carolyn stood, trying not to look impatient to get to work.

"Good morning, Carolyn," Jenna said in her sweet voice, which could alter to a growl when she read a book with a big dog or a giant in it. "I hear the team has arrived who is building you a new house."

"That's what Tony told me yesterday." Carolyn shifted uneasily, overwhelmed with the generosity. And how the thought of spending time with Michael Miller accelerated her heart rate. "There are other people who need a home as much as we do."

"I don't know what the policies are for this new group, but I've heard the MDS helps the elderly and single mothers first."

Carolyn had learned MDS stood for the Mennonite Disaster Service. The organization, which was celebrating its seventieth anniversary, had already sent people to evaluate where their volunteers could best be used, and she had sat through an uncomfortable interview. She was grateful people wanted to help her and the children. Having the community pitch in after a tragedy was what she'd been accustomed to while growing up. She was accustomed to such generosity.

What bothered her was that she wasn't a single mother. She was a single aunt.

* * *

Rubbing sleep from his eyes, Michael followed his friends into the long, low building attached to the simple white meetinghouse. The Mennonite chapel had no tower or steeple, and the windows were clear glass. He was curious about what the sanctuary looked like, but his destination, as his rumbling stomach reminded him, was breakfast in what the locals called the community center.

Rows of tables in every possible shape and size had been pushed together to allow for the most seating. Chairs and benches flanked them. Upholstered chairs were placed next to lawn chairs with plastic webbing. He wondered if every house in the village had emptied its chairs and tables into the space.

Many were filled with people intent on eating. He could understand because the aromas of eggs, bacon and toast coming from the kitchen were enticing.

As enticing as…

He halted the thought before it could form, but it wasn't easy when he noticed Carolyn Wiebe smiling at a man and a woman who were selecting generous portions of food at the window between the dining area and what looked like a well-stocked commercial kitchen. Her dark eyes sparkled like stars in a night sky, and her smile was warmer than the air billowing out of the kitchen. He found himself wishing she'd look his way.

"Over here?" asked James before Michael could wonder why he was acting like a teenage boy at his first youth singing.

Looking at where his friend was gesturing, Michael wasn't surprised none of James's brothers were seated nearby. James hadn't said anything, but it was clear he was annoyed with his three older brothers who'd swooped down from their homes in Ontario and insisted James join them in volunteering. He'd heard James had moved to Harmony Creek Hollow to get away from his family, though James had been happy when his younger sister had moved in with him earlier and now taught at the settlement's school.

Michael pushed thoughts of James's family from his head as he walked with his two friends to a round table between two rectangular ones. The three chairs on one side would work for them. He nodded to an older couple who sat on the other side before setting his hat on the table.

"The sweet rolls are fine this morning," the white-haired man said. "You'll want to check them out, but you may want to be careful." He winked and grinned before digging into his breakfast again.

Michael wasn't sure why the man had winked until he went to the serving window and saw Carolyn was handing out cinnamon rolls topped with nuts and raisins to each person who walked by. When she noticed him, she greeted him with the same smile she'd offered each person ahead of him.

"Gute mariye," he said, then said, "Good morning."

She laughed. "You don't need to translate. Anyone could guess what you were saying. After all, it didn't sound like you were asking for a second roll."

"Can we have two?" asked Benjamin from behind him.

"The rule is take all you want," she said with a smile, "but eat all you take."

Benjamin took a half step back and spooned more scrambled eggs onto his plate. When James arched a brow, he said, "Hey, I'm a growing boy."

"I'll have two rolls please, Carolyn," Michael said.

"Just remember the rules." Her smile became sassy, and he saw the resemblance between her and her son.

He couldn't keep from smiling back as their gazes met and held.

A nudge against his back broke the link between them, and Michael wasn't sure how long he'd stood there savoring her smile. He grabbed flatware rolled into a paper napkin before striding to the table.

"I told you to be careful," chided the old man with a grin as he stood and helped his wife gather their dishes. "Something sweet can knock a man right off his feet."

Michael hoped his friends hadn't heard the comments, but they laughed as they sat beside him. He bent over his plate for grace and watched from the corners of his eyes as James and Benjamin did the same.

Before they could tease him further, Michael began talking about the orientation session they were required to attend after breakfast. He didn't give either man a chance to change the subject, but he wondered why he'd bothered when he saw the grins they wore as they ate. He wasn't fooling anyone, not even himself. He looked forward to getting to know Carolyn better, but that's where he'd have to draw the line.

She was involved in her Mennonite congregation, and he had no idea if he intended to remain Amish. She didn't need to have him dump his mess of a life on her when she was trying to rebuild everything that had been lost.

She was a total mess.

But so was everyone else in Evergreen Corners.

Carolyn laughed as she thought of how Gladys Whittaker, their mayor, never used to appear in public without every hair in place. Since the flood, mud on her face seemed to be the mayor's favorite fashion accessory. Elton Hershey had had stains on his pants when he gave the sermon on Sunday. Nobody had complained about their kindhearted pastor, because everyone was fighting to get rid of mud from their clothing, too.

She squatted by the brook that had changed course. There was talk that the water would be forced back into its proper channel, but it was a low priority while people needed places to live.

Washing mud off her hands, Carolyn winced as her back reminded her of the hard work she'd done. She'd joined five others cleaning out a house that had been inundated. Once they'd gotten the mud off the floors, they spent hours removing soaked drywall before mold could grow inside the walls. She'd carried the heavy pieces of wet plaster to a pile in the yard while someone else had sprayed the two-by-fours with a mold killer.

Her hands ached as well as her elbows, shoulders and back. It'd be quicker to count the muscles that *didn't* hurt. Taking care of two children and raising chickens and baking hadn't prepared her for such physical work.

Hearing the *flap-flap* sound of a helicopter, Carolyn glanced up. It was rising from the football field behind the school. She wondered what had been delivered. She hoped fresh milk. The children were complaining about the taste of powdered milk. There were a half-dozen dairy farms on the other side of the ridge, but no way to get to them. Too many roads and bridges had been destroyed, and what would have been a ten minute drive before the flood now took hours.

She stood, holding her hands against her lower back to silence the protest from her muscles. When she saw four chickens pecking at the ground, she smiled. Mr. Aiken had told them to feel free to use whatever they found in the barn. She'd seen a bucket of corn by one stall. A couple of handfuls might draw the chickens back. That would ease the children's distress.

What Kevin and Rose Anne needed was a home. Their house hadn't been big, and most of the ancient mechanicals had needed attention she didn't know how to give. She and the children had become accustomed to faucets dripping. She'd locked off the back bedroom, fearful Kevin and Rose Anne would tumble through weak boards into the cellar. Now, the cellar hole was the sole remnant of the comfortable old house.

Seeing some broken boards heaped against stones at the brook's edge, Carolyn went to pull them out of the water, one by one. If nobody else claimed them, she could use them to build a new chicken coop.

"For all I know, Father," she said as she dropped another board on top of the two she'd pulled out, "these are what's left of my old coop. But I want them to go to whoever needs them most."

A shadow slipped over her, and Carolyn looked skyward. Was it going to rain again? Panic gripped her throat, threatening to keep her from drawing another breath.

"Would you like some help?" came a deep voice.

She turned. Michael's light-blue shirt and black suspenders weren't as filthy as her dress and apron were, and she guessed he'd come from the volunteers' orientation class. The sessions were simple, but outlined who was in charge of what and when someone should seek help before making a decision. They had ended the chaos of the first two days after the flood.

"I didn't mean to startle you," he said.

"You didn't."

"Something is upsetting you. I've seen more color in fresh snow than on your face."

She let her sore shoulders relax. "Okay, you did scare me. I was deep in my thoughts."

"This is all that's left?" He looked down into the cellar hole. "There's nothing but mud."

"Everything washed away. The furnace, the water heater and the jars of fruits and vegetables I put up in August. I haven't told the children yet. I know they aren't going to be happy with grocery store canned vegetables."

He wrinkled his nose. "Sometimes it seems you can't tell the difference between the vegetables in the can and the can itself."

"You've taken a bite out of a can?"

"Of course not." He chuckled. "You don't like exaggeration, ain't so?"

She made sure her reaction to "ain't so," a common Amish term, wasn't visible. "I'm a low-key person, Michael. I prefer to keep things simple."

"And you're exhausted."

She resisted the yearning to check her reflection in the slow waters of the brook to see how bad she looked. "I guess that's obvious."

"Why wouldn't you be tired? You were up early this morning to make breakfast for us, and now you're taking care of your chickens." His eyes narrowed as his gaze settled on the stack of wood. "Have you been pulling those out on your own?"

"I thought I could use the boards to build a chicken coop."

"A *gut* idea." Without another word, he waded into

the water. He stretched out and grabbed a board beyond her reach.

Tears flooded Carolyn's eyes as she watched him lift out the planks and set them with the others with an ease she couldn't have copied. She blinked them away. She must be more exhausted than she'd guessed.

Five minutes later, the wood was stacked. She thanked him, but he waved aside her gratitude before bending to wash his hands in the brook as she had.

"What do you call this stream?" he asked as he straightened and wiped his hands on the sides of his black broadfall trousers.

"Washboard Brook."

"Brook?" He shook his head, then pushed his brown hair back out of his eyes. "I never imagined anything called a brook could do all the damage this one has."

"I didn't, either. I don't think anyone did."

"You've never had a flood here before?"

"I've learned that if the snow up on the peaks melts really fast, we get some minor flooding. Puddles in yards and maybe a splash over onto the road where it's low." She flung out her hands. "Nothing like this."

"Have you considered leaving?"

She shook her head. "No."

"Not once?"

Wanting to be truthful—or at least partially because she couldn't mention Leland's name—rather than making believe she could endure anything nature could throw against the town, she said, "I've got to admit when I watched our home collapse and get sucked down into the water I wanted to run as fast as I could in any direction away from the flood."

"But you're still here."

"It's home."

"So you grew up here?"

Carolyn berated herself. She should have seen the direction their conversation could go and changed the topic before it touched on dangerous territory.

Knowing she must not appear to hesitate, she said, "No, but I've lived here for a while. For me, Evergreen Corners is home, and I hope it always will be."

That was a prayer she said every night before sleep, because if she had to leave, it would be in an attempt to escape from Leland Reber once and for all.

Chapter Three

The first project meeting for Carolyn's new house was scheduled for ten the next morning. Initially it had been set for eight, but she was signed up to serve breakfast. Some volunteers and government officials came in RVs, and they brought their own food. However, most arrived eager to work with tools and skills and not much else. Fortunately, fewer locals were depending on the community center's kitchen to provide their meals because some sections of town now had electricity again.

But the steady whir of generators hadn't decreased in the center of the village. Long orange extension cords snaked from the four in the school parking lot.

She stepped over the cords with care, holding Rose Anne on her hip. The little girl had woken with a sore throat. Though Carolyn suspected it was because she'd been yelling too much yesterday in games at the day care center, she agreed to the child's demands to stay with her. Kevin had been glad to have his friends to himself, and Rose Anne seemed to perk up as soon as they headed toward the school.

Carolyn reached to open the door, but a hand stretched

past her to grasp the handle. Seeing Michael and his two friends, she greeted them. She hadn't been sure if they'd be coming to the meeting, too, and she was glad to see the men who'd invited her and the children to share supper with them the previous night.

Rose Anne wiggled to get down as soon as Carolyn carried her into the school. The little girl threw her arms around one of Michael's legs and begged him for a piggyback ride.

"You don't have to do that," Carolyn told him.

He gave her a quick smile. Squatting, he waited for the child to lock her hands around his neck before he stood. He kept one arm against her to keep her steady as he loped a few yards along the hallway and back again.

"Go, horsey!" she called in excitement.

He set her on her feet, though she pleaded for another ride.

"One ride per customer," he said, tapping her freckled nose.

"Later?" Rose Anne persisted.

"Let's see what later brings." Carolyn put her hands on the child's shoulders and smiled her thanks to Michael. "I warned you offering rides to the kids last night was going to get you in trouble."

"*Gut* trouble, though."

"We'll see when all the children in town are asking for rides after you've put in a full day's work." She took Rose Anne by the hand and began walking toward the gym.

The three men followed her, talking in *Deitsch*. The words fell like precious rain on her ears, but she chatted with Rose Anne as if none of what they were saying made sense to her. She wasn't surprised the men were eager to get started. No plain man was accustomed to sitting in a classroom when work waited to be done. When she'd been growing up, every man she'd known had toiled from before sunrise to after dark. It didn't matter if the man was a farmer or had a job in one of the nearby factories or owned his own shop. Being idle wasn't part of the Amish lifestyle.

A woman Carolyn didn't know stood in front of the gym's closed double doors. Everything about her pose shouted she would tolerate no nonsense. When Carolyn said her name, the woman checked it on the clipboard she carried.

"Please wait out here," the woman said. "We're running about a half hour behind schedule."

"All right." Carolyn walked to the plastic chairs. Dropping into one, she lifted Rose Anne onto her lap. She should have borrowed a book from the day care center to keep the little girl entertained.

Michael sat next to her as his friends walked down the hall. Before she could ask, he said, "They're going to go look for something to do for the next half hour."

"You don't need to wait with us."

"The time will go faster if you've got someone to talk to."

Sliding Rose Anne off her lap when her niece began to wiggle, Carolyn told her to stay in sight. The little girl nodded and began to jump from one black tile to the next on the checkered floor.

"I appreciate you staying here, but it's not necessary," Carolyn said, keeping her eyes on the child who could scurry away like a rabbit running from a dog. "I'm not sure I want the time to go faster."

"Nervous?" Disbelief deepened his voice. "Why? These people are here to help you."

"It's not easy to ask others for help."

"I get that." He leaned back, crossed his arms over his chest and stretched his long legs out, much to Rose Anne's delight as she began to leap over them. "But you've got to think about your *kinder*—I mean, your children."

"They're pretty much all I think about." She wondered why it was so easy to be honest with Michael, whom she hadn't known two days ago. "I'd do anything to make sure they've got a safe place to live."

"Even deal with bureaucrats?" He reached out to steady Rose Anne when she almost tripped over his boots.

Carolyn smiled. "When you put it that way, going through this meeting isn't too much to ask, is it?"

"Only you can answer that."

"I thought I did."

His laugh resonated down the otherwise empty hall. "Do you always speak plainly?"

"No."

"I guess I should feel honored."

"I guess you should." She was about to add more, then realized the little girl was partway around a corner. Calling Rose Anne back, she said, "I shouldn't have given in to her make-believe sore throat this morning. I should have insisted she stay at day care." She crooked a finger at her niece who was edging toward the end of the hall again. "They're accustomed to having me around, especially Rose Anne. She's been going to nursery school, but it's not the same as being left at the day care center all day, every day."

"So she convinced you to let her come with you."

"She didn't have to try hard." She held out her hand,

and her niece ran over to take it. "I like spending time with my Rosie Annie."

The little girl giggled as she leaned on Carolyn's knee. "I'm sweat smelling, like a rose. That's what Mommy always says."

"Maybe not always, but you do smell *sweet* today." She ruffled the child's silken hair. Rose Anne had no memories of her real mother, and Kevin seemed to have forgotten Carolyn was his aunt. She thanked God every morning and night for that, though she prayed there would come a time when she could be honest. "Last night, you were dirty. It took a while to get you clean so you smelled as sweet as a rose again." To Michael, who was grinning at how Rose Anne had called herself "sweat smelling," she added, "We're pretty much limited to a bucket of water each."

"When can I take a big-girl bath again?" Rose Anne's voice became a whine. "I miss my bath tube and my floatie fishies."

She means bathtub, Carolyn mouthed so Michael could read her lips. When he nodded his understanding, she said aloud, "I can't tell you when, but it'll be…" She didn't want to give the child a specific date because she didn't have any idea how long it would take to build their new house. And she didn't want to talk about the plastic toys Rose Anne called her floatie fishies. They had washed away with everything in the house.

Michael stood, then dropped to one knee beside her niece. That brought his eyes almost level with Rose Anne's. "I can tell you when your new house and new bathtub will be ready. It's going to be right after Christmas."

"Christmas is a looooooooong time away," Rose Anne argued.

"No, it's not. Today is October twenty-fifth, so Christmas is exactly two months away." Holding up two fingers, he lowered first one, then the other. "One-two. See? Quick like a bunny."

"That's what Mommy says. Quick like a bunny!" Rose Anne bounced with excitement. "Mr. Michael knows quick like a bunny, too."

"I know." As the little girl danced and twirled along the hall, Carolyn asked, "'Mr. Michael?'"

"One of the ladies working at supper last night called me that, and the kids started using it."

"You're good with children. Do you have any?"

"No, but my brother has year-old twins, and there are plenty of kids in our settlement." He surveyed the hall before adding, "My brother has his life set for him…as you do."

She was amazed at his wistful tone. Michael had seemed so sure of himself. Was there a tragedy in his past, too, or did he have another reason to envy his brother's choices in life?

The woman who'd stood by the gym doors came out and called, "Carolyn Wiebe? They're ready for you."

A shiver of anxiety trilled down her back, but Carolyn stood. When Rose Anne rushed to her side, she wasn't sure if the little girl was aware of her agitation or wanted a change of scenery after exploring every inch of the hall. Carolyn glanced at Michael who'd gotten up, too, and she knew she wasn't hiding her nerves from him.

But he didn't offer her trite consolation. Instead, he motioned for her to lead the way.

In the gym, four round tables with plenty of chairs had been placed between the two sets of bleachers. Mats remained under the basketball hoops. Rose Anne took off her shoes and ran to join the other children playing on them.

"The *kinder* are having *gut* fun," Michael said as the woman led them toward the most distant table.

Carolyn recognized fellow residents who'd lost their homes, and she guessed the others were volunteers like Michael and his friends. To avoid any chance of eavesdropping on their conversations, she replied, "The kids are having more fun now than we had the first night after the flood. For lots of us, those mats were our beds. We were so exhausted we would have slept on the wood floor."

"Glen," the woman with the clipboard said, "here's your client. Carolyn Wiebe."

Trying not to bristle at the woman's tone that suggested Carolyn was an unworthy charity case, she was glad when the woman walked away.

"I'm Glen Landis," said the man who was as thin as the hair across his pate. "The project director."

"We've met," Carolyn replied, pulling her tattered composure around her like a comfortable blanket. "About a year and a half ago, you came to speak at the Evergreen Corners Mennonite Meetinghouse about your experiences."

"In the recovery efforts after Hurricanes Katrina and Harvey?" He smiled as Michael's two friends jogged across the gym to join them. From his speech, she'd learned he considered rebuilding homes and communities his mission work. "Those were overwhelming experiences. I've been told you've met some of the people who'll be working on your house."

"I've met Benjamin, James and Michael." She looked at each man as she said his name. Only belatedly did she realize how foolish she'd been to speak Michael's name last. Without an excuse to shift away, her gaze lingered on him.

Michael gave her a bolstering smile, and she wished she could fling her arms around him as Rose Anne had. She hadn't realized how much she needed someone's support.

"Here comes the rest of the crew," Glen said, motioning for everyone to take a seat.

He went around the table, introducing each person. Art Kennel was the man who looked like a jolly grandfather. Jose Lopez was almost as lanky as Glen and taller. The sole woman was Trisha Lehman. She had the same no-nonsense air about her as the woman by the door, but her smile put Carolyn at ease.

After leading them in prayer to thank God for His grace in bringing them together, Glen pulled a stack of pages stapled on one side out of a briefcase by his chair. He put them in front of Carolyn.

"This is our standard house plan." He glanced around the table. "Several of you have already built one or more of these houses. If you haven't or you want to examine the plans more closely, get a copy from me after this meeting."

She stared at the simple house with a living room, kitchen, a bath and two bedrooms. It wasn't as big as her previous house, but it would be more than sufficient for what she and the children needed.

As if she'd spoken aloud, Glen said, "Carolyn, if you see things you want to have changed, now is the time to tell us."

"What sort of things?" She thought of the house the

water had taken from her. That rundown house had been their home, something that couldn't be drawn on paper.

"I know you have two children, a girl and a boy. If you want a third bedroom, so each child may have their own—something I've been told by my own kids is an absolute necessity—we can add one. It's possible to get a second bathroom, but it'll depend on the amount of money raised through donors and what you can contribute."

"Definitely the extra bedroom, but one bathroom will suffice."

"That we should be able to provide within the budget we've been given." He opened a bright blue folder and wrote some notes before launching into an explanation of what each of the six pages in the plans contained.

Carolyn tried to take in the information on septic systems and wells and the required number of electric outlets and where a stackable washer and dryer could be put if she wanted to keep the coat closet by the front door and a linen cupboard in the bathroom. Her head spun with numbers and dimensions, and she was relieved when Glen reassured her they'd be revisiting the plans every day on the work site and once a week in the gym.

"The first supplies will be delivered this afternoon," he announced as he refolded the plans. "We hope to start on your house within days. It'll depend on the weather, of course."

"I understand." Looking around the table, she said, "Thank you, everyone. Your kindness humbles me. You make me want to live *Hebrews* 13:2 'Be not forgetful to entertain strangers: for thereby some have entertained angels unawares.' My door will always be open to you." She laughed. "Once I have a door, that is."

The others joined in her laughter, and Michael took her

hand under the table and squeezed it. A sense of comfort filled her at his compassion.

"Oh, one more thing," Glen said. "We've asked the press to stay away, but we hope you'll agree to a short interview, Carolyn, after we have the blessing for your new home. We've found seeing how others have worked with us leads to more people offering to volunteer. Everyone wants to be part of a happy ending to what started out as a sad story."

Carolyn stiffened. "An interview?"

"Nothing complicated. A short film to put on our website to show donors how they've helped."

Horror pulsed through every vein in her body, like the flood waters closing in around her again, only this time with fire atop of the rushing waves. She shook her head.

"Is that a problem?" asked Glen.

She pushed back her chair. "If doing an interview is a condition for your help, I can't do this."

"You don't want our help?"

Wishing she didn't have to see the shock on these kind faces, she wondered how much more appalled they'd be if she told them the truth of why she was turning down their offer. Would any of them have been able to comprehend the depth of fear stalking her in the form of Leland Reber?

"No," she whispered.

Michael came to his feet along with everyone else at the table when Carolyn stood and, taking Rose Anne by the hand as the little girl protested she needed to retrieve her shoes, started for the door. Unlike everyone else who seemed frozen in shock, he couldn't watch her throw away her future. Didn't she realize how blessed she was to know what future she wanted?

As he strode after her, he was surprised to feel a pinch

of vexation. Her future was assured if she agreed to the terms set out by Amish Helping Hands' partners. She could enjoy a comfortable life with her *kinder* among her friends, neighbors and congregation. It was being handed to her, and she was turning her back on it.

How he envied her for having the chance to have the life she wanted! Nobody could offer him that, because he didn't know how he wished his future to unfurl.

He blocked Carolyn's path to the door. She started to walk around him, but he edged to the side, halting her.

"Are you out of your mind?" he asked, not caring that everyone in the gym was staring at him and Carolyn. He bent and whispered to Rose Anne to go play with the other *kinder*. As the little girl skipped across the gym, he looked at her *mamm*. "Your *kinder* can't live the rest of their lives in a barn."

"I don't want to be interviewed."

"If you're shy—" he began, though he couldn't believe that was the case. She'd been outgoing when he'd arrived.

"I don't want to be interviewed."

"Tell Glen that. I'm sure he can find someone else to talk to the reporters."

"It's not just being interviewed. I don't want anyone taking our pictures."

He frowned. "I thought the Mennonites were more liberal than we Amish are. When I first saw the news about the damage here, there were plenty of pictures of people gathered at your meetinghouse."

"I don't want it. Can't that be answer enough?"

His first inclination was to say no, but seeing how distraught she was, he relented. He couldn't help being curious why Carolyn—who'd been calm and rational yesterday—found such a simple request upsetting.

"Let me talk to Glen. You and your cute kids would provide great promotional material for them, but I'm sure he can find someone else who's willing to be the focus of the article."

She whispered her thanks, then began to apologize. When he stood near her, he was surprised how tiny she was. Her personality and heart were so big that she seemed to tower over others around her. Now she appeared broken. He wasn't sure why, but he must halt her from making a huge mistake.

"No, Carolyn. There's no need to ask for forgiveness. Not mine, anyhow, but you need to be honest with Glen and the rest of the team. They deserve to know how you feel."

She lifted her chin and drew in a deep breath. "You're right."

"It's been known to happen every once in a while." His attempt at humor gained him the faintest of smiles from her, but it was enough for him to know she'd made up her mind to negotiate for what she had to have.

When they returned to the table where the other volunteers had left Glen sitting alone, the project director had closed the blue folder.

Michael felt his stomach clench. Did that mean Glen would be shutting down work on Carolyn's house, too? Michael didn't want to believe that, but he knew little about *Englisch* ways.

Pulling out a chair, Glen motioned for Carolyn to sit. He gave Michael a pointed look over her head, but Michael decided not to take the hint and allow the two to speak alone.

"I'm sorry to distress you," Glen said in a subdued voice.

"I'm sorry I tried to storm out of here," she whispered. "I

can't—I don't want to be interviewed or have the children interviewed. I understand if you can't build us a house."

Michael saw his own questions on Glen's face. Carolyn had used the word *can't*. Why couldn't she be interviewed? What was she trying to hide about herself and the *kinder*?

"Of course we're going to build your house," Glen replied. "We'd love to have you and the children be part of the information we share with possible volunteers and donors, but that's not a requirement for you. I'm sorry if I gave you that impression."

"Don't blame yourself," she said, once more with the quiet composure Michael admired. "I'm on edge. If someone says boo, I'll jump high enough to hit my head on the clouds."

Glen laughed. "We'll keep that in mind when we're ready to put the roof on your house. We wouldn't want you to go right through it the first day."

Fifteen minutes later, Michael stood in the hall with his friends from Harmony Creek Hollow while Carolyn knelt nearby, tying Rose Anne's bright red and yellow sneakers. He spoke in *Deitsch*. Benjamin and James, peppering him with questions about why Carolyn had reacted as she had and if the project was moving forward, used the same language. He didn't want Carolyn to know they were talking about her, though he guessed she had some suspicion of that because she glanced in their direction a couple of times. He told his friends he wasn't sure what had bothered her.

"We might never know," he said.

"Women," grumbled Benjamin. "One thing I learned from my sister is it's impossible to guess what they're thinking. I've figured out it's better not to try."

James nodded. "I guess that's why we're bachelors."

Michael changed the subject to the next day when they'd start loading building materials onto a donated forklift and moving them to the construction site.

"It'll take us at least a day to get the forms set up and ready for concrete," Benjamin added.

"Do we have tarps to protect the supplies from rain and mud?"

"I saw some among the pallets of supplies." James scratched behind his ear as he mused, "There are three houses being started at the same time. I wonder if we've got enough supplies."

"Let's not look for trouble before we find it," Michael replied, clapping his friend on the shoulder.

"Thanks for coming today," Carolyn said as she walked past them. "I'm sorry for the scene I caused. Let me make it up to you. I'll have the keys for the forklift waiting for you at supper so you can get a good start in the morning. See you there."

Michael stared after her. They'd been talking in *Deitsch*. Yet, Carolyn had spoken about the forklift as if she'd understood everything they'd said.

How was that possible?

Looking at his friends, he saw the same consternation on their faces.

"*Deitsch* isn't so different from German," James said. "If she's fluent in German, she'd get the gist of our conversation."

"*Ja.*" Michael didn't add more.

But if his friend wasn't right, it meant one thing: Carolyn Wiebe might not be what she appeared to be.

Chapter Four

Michael quietly shut the door to the trailer he was sharing with his friends from Harmony Creek Hollow and stepped out into the cold morning. He didn't want to wake Benjamin or James or anyone else who might be asleep in the other travel trailer parked behind the used car dealership. The two trailers had been donated for the workers rebuilding the homes. He hadn't expected anything so comfortable when he'd volunteered.

Though describing the cramped trailer as comfortable wasn't accurate. With three full-grown men trying to squeeze past each other as they got ready each morning and went to bed each night for the past three days, it was a tight squeeze. However, the narrow bed where he slept had a *gut* mattress.

He looked at his trousers. They were his next-to-last clean pair. The local laundromat had told volunteers that as soon as the business was open in a couple of weeks, they were welcome to come in anytime to wash their clothes for free. Something in the water had left a dirty line above the tops of his rubber boots. The scum might have been gasoline or fuel oil or some other chemical that had leaked into the brook after the flood swept cars and furnaces and everything else along it. He hadn't seen the telltale rainbow sheen, but it might have dissipated enough so it was no longer visible.

The volunteers working in the flooded houses had been given white plastic coveralls as well as ventilating masks. Mold had begun growing as the water receded, so those workers had to be protected when they tore out drenched drywall and tossed the pieces into wheelbarrows that were then taken to big dumpsters sitting at a central spot in town. The plan, as he understood it, had been for the debris to be removed daily, but so far nobody had come to retrieve it. Stacks of reeking building materials and furniture and carpet were piled along the streets.

The rumble of generators came from the village. He walked past a collection of used cars marked with bright orange paint. When he'd asked why, he'd been told the cars would be destroyed. Water was as destructive to an internal combustion engine as it was to a wooden structure.

Michael counted more than two dozen buildings with visible damage before he stopped, knowing there were more with ruined interior walls and drenched contents. Grimacing, he guessed anything in those buildings wore the same dark sheen as whatever stained his trousers.

What a mess! Before he arrived he hadn't imagined the breadth of the disaster.

There was one thought he hadn't been able to shake out of his head as he stared at the brightly colored trees on the mountain beyond the village. If the storm had blasted its way up the other side of the Green Mountains, the settlement along Harmony Creek could have been washed away.

God, make use of my hands and my arms and what-ever else You need to help these people regain their nor-mal lives. Let my heart be as eager to help here as it would be to do the same for those at home.

He prayed something similar every morning when he went on a short walk before breakfast. He depended on the prayer to focus him on the work ahead of him. Talk-ing to God also helped him clear his mind of thoughts that seemed to center around the enigma Carolyn was. She'd never explained why she'd reacted so vehemently when Glen spoke about an interview.

Shoving his hands into his pockets, Michael contin-ued toward the village. How had Carolyn coped with this day after day for the past week? Nobody could have been prepared for what had occurred, but except for the single outburst at the school, she'd been calm. He was a bit envious because he wished he knew how she managed the drama surrounding her. Maybe if he could learn how she did it, he'd be able to do it himself.

Michael didn't meet anyone else as he walked past the library. The large two-story building was solid on its foundation, or at least the stone walls made it appear that way. He couldn't say the same for the seafood res-taurant next door. The whole building listed to the right, revealing the foundation had been compromised. Several other structures along the street were also off-kilter, one two-story house so tilted the eaves on one side were low enough he could have touched them without rising to his toes. Yellow police tape surrounded the house, a warn-ing that it might collapse.

The odor of mildew strengthened as he continued along the street. Raw earth scents rose from where trees had been ripped from the ground, leaving gaping holes and thick fingers of roots torn apart. Broken flowerpots lay shattered by front steps, but he guessed they'd once been much farther upstream.

The nearer he got to the brook the worse the damage was. He slowed to stare at the remnants of one house where the first floor had vanished. The upper story sat on the ground about ten feet from the foundation. Another house was tipped over, every window and door intact, as if a gigantic hand had reached down and lifted it off its foundation before setting it on the ground. Not far away, a clock perched over a shop's door. Its hands marked the time the flood had struck the building.

6:47.

As Carolyn had said, if the waters had arrived a few hours later, people would have been in bed and might not have had time to escape.

Michael sent up a prayer of thanks for the lives saved through God's providence. Many villagers had lost everything, but they had their most precious possessions—their lives and their families' lives.

What stopped him in his tracks, however, was the sight of the covered bridge on the north side of the village. One half hung precariously over the water. The rest of it had vanished except for a pair of boards. The top of each arch was more than twelve feet off the ground, and he tried to imagine water reaching high enough to tear the bridge apart.

Destruction spread to the horizon on both sides of a brook he could have waded across in a half-dozen steps. Trees were lying on their sides, on the ground or propped on top of broken roofs. Water pooled everywhere. He'd been wandering through this disaster for three days and still hadn't seen the full extent of the destruction.

"Can't believe your eyes, can you?" asked James as he came to stand beside him. His stained pants were stuffed into the tops of his boots. He held out a cup of *kaffi* to Michael.

Taking the cup with a nod of gratitude, he answered, "I can't get accustomed to the randomness of it all." He pointed along the brook toward where a garden shed sat on an island, separated from its house by ten feet of water. "Both buildings look fine, but Washboard Brook now runs between them instead of behind the shed as I assume it used to."

"I've heard there are plans to put the brook back into its original banks."

"I've heard that, too, but I'm not sure if the state will go to the expense of reconnecting a house and its shed."

"Then it may be left to the homeowner to reroute the water."

Michael arched his brows, knowing such a task would require excavating equipment and permits. Maybe some rules would be relaxed for the rebuilding, but he guessed most would be kept in place to protect the village and its inhabitants from a repeat of the disaster.

For the first time he wondered how long it would take Evergreen Corners to return to normal.

Or if it ever would.

At breakfast, Michael had had a chance to greet Carolyn and receive one of her pretty smiles, but he didn't have time to say anything more before he had to move on to let others get their food. It was long enough for him to notice the dark circles under her eyes, and he wondered what had kept her awake. The *kinder*? The house? Something else?

Pondering the questions kept him silent through breakfast. He was quiet as he walked with James and Benjamin and the other volunteers toward where they'd be clearing debris from the site of Carolyn's house. At least, he told himself, they could reassure her the project was moving forward.

Jose shared apples from his orchard. The man was one of the hardest workers at the site, and Michael wasn't surprised to learn Jose had volunteered at other disasters throughout New England. Each day, he came with a treat to share. Though Jose said the apples had been harvested a few weeks ago, they had a crispness that put any apple Michael had ever had in Pennsylvania to shame.

"Our weather in Vermont is perfect for apples," Jose said. "Warm summer days with cooler nights. When we get plenty of rain—" He scowled as if he'd found a worm in the core of the apple he was eating. "I mean *regular* rain, not flooding rain like they had along these valleys. When we get lots of nice, steady rain, the apples are juicy. After drier summers like this one, the apples aren't as juicy, but they're sweeter. Either way, they're great for eating, cooking and making cider."

Trisha, who'd worked with him in the past, laughed. "You sound like an ad for the Vermont apple growers' association."

"Hey, a guy's got to be proud of what he does." He turned to the other men. "Right?"

Michael hastened to agree rather than explain pride— *hochmut*—was seen as a negative among the Amish. He doubted the *Englischers* would be interested in hearing about plain life, and he didn't want to cause any sort of gulf between the plain volunteers and the *Englisch* ones.

He glanced at his friends and gave the slightest shrug. He got grins in return.

Noise met them before they reached the remains of Carolyn's home. Generators rumbled, waiting for electric tools to be connected to them. The sound of circular saws battled the whir of gas-powered chainsaws cutting through the debris blocking the brook, creating pools where there shouldn't be any. Small clouds of blue-gray smoke marked each spot where someone was slicing through wood that might once have been a house or a fence.

As they emerged from the trees separating her property from her neighbor's, large land-moving equipment was being maneuvered toward Carolyn's cellar hole. The tons of gravel deposited by the swollen brook onto her yard crunched under large tires and caterpillar tracks. Two skid steers, which looked like a *kind*'s toys compared to the massive vehicles, were shoving fallen trees into a pile near the brook. He knew they would be burned later but were being shifted out of the way so the massive equipment could do its work.

Glen Landis stood near stone steps that had led to the house. From there, he could supervise workers removing the debris, filling in the old cellar hole and laying out the new foundation. Michael and James were put to work marking the location of the new house with sticks and bright orange string while the others focused on finishing the cleanup.

When the evaluation had come back on Carolyn's house the day before yesterday, the decision had been clear. The old house, as Michael had suspected, had been built too close to the brook. Though it'd been almost twenty yards away, the building hadn't been spared during what people were calling a thousand-year flood. He didn't have much confidence in their timetable. The flood caused by Hurricane Kevin had been the fifth in the past hundred years.

Michael wondered if Carolyn had been consulted about the new location, which would set the front porch a few yards from the road. She had around six acres on either side of the brook, but most was wooded, so putting the house near its original location seemed the best idea.

Though he was focused on his task of trying to make a perfect rectangle with James's help, Michael knew the instant Carolyn arrived in the clearing. Some sense he couldn't name told him she was nearby. He couldn't keep from smiling. She had a white crocheted shawl over the shoulders of the pink dress that looked to be far too big for her. It had, he guessed, come from the bins of donated clothing. She'd cinched it with a black apron, accenting her slender waist. Her gold locket twinkled around her neck.

She scanned the work site and smiled. That expression softened when her gaze caressed his, pausing for a single heartbeat before moving on. Was it his imagination that her smile had grown a shade warmer when their eyes connected?

"Is this the spot for the next stake?" James asked in an impatient tone that suggested he'd already posed the question once or twice.

Michael concentrated on his task. As much as he enjoyed looking at Carolyn, he couldn't let his attention wander. He squatted and placed a laser level on the ground so the red line marked where the next few stakes should be driven.

His sleeve was grabbed, and he struggled to hold his

balance in the awkward stance. Putting his hands on the dirt, he pushed himself to his feet when he realized Carolyn must have rushed down to them.

"Was iss letz?" he asked. When she opened her mouth, he said in *Englisch*, "What's wrong?"

A flurry of emotions stormed across her face before she looked away to point farther down the hillside. "Where's the wood we pulled out of the brook?"

He squinted through the bright morning sunshine. "Right there." As he was about to add more, a skid steer moved toward the stack. The forks started to slide under the wood. "Did you tell them to move it?"

"No."

Running at a pace that threatened to send him falling face-first, he managed to slide to a stop before he reached the one-man forklift.

The man inside was so riveted on his task, he didn't see Michael waving his arms. Michael leaped forward and grabbed the end of one of the boards rising on the forklift.

A curse battered his ears, but he ignored it as he motioned to the man controlling the skid steer.

"Are you crazy?" demanded the man, poking his head out of the small vehicle.

"The owner wants to hold on to these boards."

"Why?" asked the operator. "She's getting a brand-new house."

"She collected them to rebuild her chicken coop." He pointed toward where a half-dozen chickens were pecking at the ground near where an old tree trunk had been removed. A feast of bugs and worms must have been uncovered.

"Those chickens aren't going to be long for this world

if they keep wandering around here. Nobody's going to be watching for them." The operator gave a twisted grin. "They're gonna be flat chickens in no time."

Michael knew the guy was right. "I'll take care of them."

"They're in the way."

"Okay." He held up one hand. "I'll be back in five minutes."

The man switched off the skid steer. "I'll wait here." His tone suggested Michael was wasting everyone's time defending a pile of water-soaked wood and a few chickens.

Striding up the hill, Michael explained what the skid steer operator had told him.

"I'll talk to Glen." Carolyn walked away before anyone could reply.

Michael turned to his friends. "We've got a new job."

"What's that?" asked James, stretching as Michael had done a few minutes ago.

"How are you at catching chickens?"

Benjamin groaned. "Don't tell us you volunteered *us* to round up Carolyn's chickens."

"All right, I won't tell you, but let's go. We need to get them before—" He grinned when a chicken let out an ear-splitting squawk as it flapped away from a bulldozer, leaving a cloud of feathers and dust in its wake. "I, for one, don't want to explain to Carolyn and her *kinder* why their chickens have gone bald."

With a laugh, the men went to capture the hens. It wasn't the day Michael had planned, but he'd already learned, despite the plans Glen and his team had made, there were going to be plenty of surprises while rebuilding Carolyn's house.

* * *

Carolyn scrubbed the last of the muffin tins from breakfast in the community center's kitchen. She'd returned to work there after being reassured by Glen that her small pile of boards would be kept safe so she could build another chicken coop.

During the walk to the community center, she hadn't been able to keep from smiling as she thought of Michael taking off at top speed to stop the skid steer operator from tossing them onto the pile with the rest of the debris. If the ground had been covered by snow, he would have looked like a reckless snowboarder on Mount Snow.

Yet, he'd saved the boards, and she appreciated his interceding on her behalf. He seemed to be a *gut* man.

But so did Leland when you first met him.

She shuddered at the thought of her brother-in-law and her own father, who'd derided her mother every chance he had. Others had acted as if they admired both Leland and her father. Others who hadn't seen the truth hidden by charming smiles. She didn't want to believe Michael was the same, but she'd be a fool to leave herself and Kevin and Rose Anne vulnerable to another man.

He wouldn't be in Evergreen Corners for long— another reason not to get too close to him. She'd keep her distance.

Just in case.

"Hey! Guess what? There are more Amish folks here."

Carolyn's ears perked up at the words spoken by someone on the far side of the community kitchen.

More Amish? A shiver of dismay sliced through her. What if Leland had secreted himself among these plain people and come to Evergreen Corners with them? What if she was recognized as Cora Hilty from Indiana?

She put the last muffin tray in the drainer and squeezed out the dishrag. Draping it over the faucet, she said, "I'll be right back."

The other women looked at her in obvious confusion.

She gave them a wide smile and whirled to leave before someone could ask a question she'd have to evade as she had so many others. When she had embarked on this new life, she hadn't given any thought to how hard it would be to protect the truth from those she called friends. So many times when she'd stopped to chat with Jenna in the library, she'd been tempted to spill everything.

But the burden was hers and hers alone until Kevin and Rose Anne were old enough to be told the truth. She tried not to let herself think about what their reactions would be.

When Carolyn emerged from the community center and hurried to the center of the village, she saw four plain people standing in the middle of the green and looking around as if they didn't know what to do first. The three men, all wearing black hats, were bachelors because none had beards. The lone woman had a black bonnet over her *kapp* and wore a black wool coat, so Carolyn couldn't guess which community they came from. A single suitcase and three paper grocery bags sat on the ground by their feet.

"Can I help you?" Carolyn asked as she reached the quartet.

"We're here to help," said the tallest man. "Do you know where we go to meet with the project director?"

"The high school." She smiled. "I'll show you the way. I'm Carolyn Wiebe, by the way."

"Isaac Kauffman," the tall man answered. "This is my sister Abby, and our cousins, Danny and Vernon Umble."

Danny appeared younger than the others, not much more than a teenager, while Vernon looked the oldest of the foursome, probably in his early forties. He wore thick glasses that perched on the end of his nose. As Carolyn greeted them, he pushed up his glasses, but they slid down again when he reached for one of the paper bags.

The cousins fell in step behind Carolyn and the Kauffmans as she led them across the green. She kept her sigh of relief silent when they told her they were the only ones from their community able to spare time to help with the rebuilding.

"Ours is a newer settlement," Abby said with a friendly smile. "In the Northeast Kingdom."

Carolyn knew the term as everyone who lived in Vermont did. The Northeast Kingdom consisted of the counties abutting Canada and New Hampshire.

"I hadn't heard about any Amish in Vermont."

Abby smiled. "We don't broadcast we're here."

Flustered, Carolyn hurried to reassure the woman she knew enough about Old Order Amish to understand they wouldn't make a big deal out of the monumental task of building a new settlement. She sighed. Walking the fine line between pretending she was curious about the Amish and yet disguising how much she knew was becoming more difficult. Mennonites and *Englischers* never seemed to notice when she revealed a fact only someone who'd lived a plain life would know. Nobody had questioned— not once—what sort of community she'd lived in before she came to Evergreen Corners.

As more Amish arrived to assist, she needed to be more cautious, or the fragile house of cards she'd built would tumble down and make her and the children more vulnerable to being found by Leland. She must curb her tongue before she destroyed what she'd created over the past four years.

"How do you like Vermont?" Carolyn asked, knowing she mustn't get lost in her thoughts and make the newcomers curious about *her*.

"The winters are much colder than we had in Pennsylvania." Abby gave an exaggerated shiver.

Carolyn's smile became more sincere. "Is everyone in your settlement from Pennsylvania?"

"So far."

"That's nice. You've got a sense of community from where you lived before." She pushed aside her ever-present fear that the newcomers were from Indiana and might recognize her.

She hoped those blessings would continue, and she wouldn't find herself face-to-face with Leland Reber when she least expected it. She wasn't sure what he'd do, but she was certain of what she would. She'd take the children and flee again, leaving everything and everyone else behind.

Chapter Five

Michael hoped nobody else could hear his stomach grumbling. The midday meal was more than an hour away, but his gut wasn't ready to be rational. He was hungry and another of Jose's apples had only taken the edge off those pangs.

But right now, he needed to find someone named Isaac Kauffman. Glen had said the man with the skills of a master mason should have arrived today in Evergreen Corners. No more work could be done on any of the houses until Isaac reviewed the dimensions of the foundations and approved them. Isaac had worked on other projects with Glen, who'd come to depend on his expertise.

Michael looked across the village green, a small open park with a veterans' memorial stone at one end and a damaged gazebo big enough to hold a band at the other. Over by the high school, he saw Carolyn with people he hadn't seen before. Their clothing announced they were Lancaster County Amish.

When she laughed, he admired how she seemed to take each challenge as it came and maintained her positive attitude. He'd seen dismay shadowing her eyes and knew she was haunted by the flood, yet she made an effort to put everyone around her at ease.

What would she say if he told her what *he* had been thinking while working today? Would she be shocked he wanted to talk to her about living and worshipping as a Mennonite? God might have brought him to Evergreen Corners to give him a chance to consider his future without input from well-meaning friends and family. Even if he chose not to be baptized as a member of the *Leit*, he wanted to live a plain life. He knew nothing about the day-to-day lives of other plain sects or how they praised God in their churches. He'd always attended services in a neighbor's house.

But now wasn't the time to ask his questions. Not when she stood with an Amish woman and three plain men.

Michael smiled when Carolyn motioned for him to join her and the others. She introduced him to the Kauffmans and the Umble brothers. He learned they'd come from northeastern Vermont, where a Pennsylvania daughter settlement had been established.

When Isaac switched to *Deitsch*, Michael wanted to chuckle at the choice of topic. Deciding which family or friends they might have in common was the Amish way of meeting new folks. Somewhere along the line, everyone shared ancestors.

Glancing at Carolyn, he saw her brow was ruffled in concentration as she listened to them. Was she trying to pick out words she understood? Or did she comprehend more than a few words? She'd seemed to know what he and his friends were talking about when they spoke in *Deitsch* at the school.

"Glen has been waiting for you to arrive, Isaac," Michael said after they'd established they had a common ancestor six generations back.

"How many foundations are you preparing?" asked the man who was taller than James. His light brown hair was streaked with blond from hours of working outside.

"Three."

Isaac laughed. "Glen likes to keep lots of balls in the air at one time. I keep telling him it would be more efficient to start one house, finish the first step of it and then start the next house."

"Like singing a round?"

"*Ja*. Exactly." He switched to *Englisch* with a guilty glance toward Carolyn. "I'd best check in with Glen."

"I hope he'll give us a chance to move in before bedtime," grumbled Vernon. The older man took off his black hat, revealing a balding pate that glistened in the sunlight.

When the newcomers went into the school, Carolyn said she needed to return to the community center. Michael walked with her because he should get back to the building site and let Glen know Isaac had arrived.

But he had another matter on his mind. "Do you speak German?"

Her dark brown eyes widened. "That's an odd question."

"I was watching you while Isaac and the others spoke. You seemed focused on every word." He was bumbling through what should have been simple. "You looked like you were trying to puzzle out what we were saying."

"I could understand names. There were a lot. Do you know all those people you named?"

"Some I know. Some the Kauffmans and the Umbles know. A few we both know or know of."

"That's amazing! You live in New York State, and they live on the Canadian border. Yet you have friends in common."

"All of us have roots in Lancaster County, Pennsylvania."

Her face became less tense as the hint of a smile brushed her lips. "Ah, I get it."

"And you didn't understand anything but the names?"

She bent to pick up a paper cup and tossed it into a nearby trash barrel. Wiping her hands, she said, "Some words sounded like English. If I offended you by listening, I'm sorry."

"Of course you didn't offend."

"I'm glad." She gave him a smile, and his heart lurched in his chest. "I can't ever forget what you and the others are doing for us. I wouldn't want to make you think I was unappreciative."

"Why do you think we'd feel that way?"

She shrugged, her smile losing a bit of its brilliance. "I know…that is, I've heard… People have told me the Amish like to keep separate from the world. I didn't want you to think I was trying to intrude."

"Will it make you feel better if I tell you I'll let you know if you do anything to offend me?"

"Yes!"

He laughed at her sudden enthusiasm. When she looked at him as if he'd lost his mind right in front of her, he hurried to say, "I was teasing you, Carolyn. You've got enough to worry about without worrying you might be crossing some imaginary line."

"If you're sure…"

"I'm sure." He patted her shoulder as he would have

his brother when he wanted to assure Gabriel of something.

But the tingles scurrying along his arm were nothing he'd ever felt with his brother.

Or anyone else…not even Adah.

The memory of the woman who'd played him for a *dummkopf* and then left him for another man in front of all their friends was like a bucket of icy reality poured over his head. He'd decided at that moment to expel any kind of drama from his life, and he had.

Until now, when he'd come alive as never before with a chaste touch.

He turned away, mumbling about seeing Carolyn later at the building site. If she replied or if she went on her way without any reaction was something he'd never know because he didn't look back as he walked away.

How could he have forgotten the incident when Adah had paraded her new boyfriend in front of him so she could squeeze as much drama out of the situation as possible? He'd begun to question everything in his life. If he could be so wrong about Adah, how could he be certain of anything else?

It was something he couldn't allow himself to forget again.

Sleep refused to come.

Carolyn tossed and turned and punched her pillow, searching for a comfortable place on it. The pillowcase seemed too wrinkled, or when she tried to pull it tight, it puffed, striking her in the nose. When she finally got comfortable, her right cheek itched. She gave in to the need to scratch it, and the process of finding a good spot on the pillow began all over again.

More than once, she considered getting up and walking around until she was so tired she would collapse into bed and sleep. She couldn't do that without risking waking the children and the others in the stables.

There were now only two other families with them. The rest had been able to return home or had moved in with relatives. She and Kevin and Rose Anne didn't have kinfolk in Evergreen Corners. As far as she knew, she wasn't related to anyone in the whole state of Vermont.

She tried not to think of the *aentis* and *onkels* and cousins in Indiana who might still be wondering where she and the children were. Tears swelled into her eyes when the *Deitsch* words came into her thoughts. *Aenti* and *onkel* were two words that once had been as common as breathing. Though Carolyn missed her life in Indiana, she had turned her back on it, never expecting to encounter an Amish person again.

Then the flood swept everything away and good-hearted volunteers came to help.

Amish volunteers.

Michael's face filled her mind along with a pulse of guilt. She couldn't blame him for leaving abruptly when they'd been talking on the village green. In her efforts to pretend she didn't know about *Deitsch*, she'd sounded ludicrous.

Why didn't you say that you spoke German even though you don't?

The answer was simple. She didn't want to lie, though she was avoiding the truth every day. However, she had a good reason. She was protecting the children from their brutal father. Being dishonest with Michael about understanding German wouldn't have done anything to prevent

Leland from finding her and the children, so she couldn't bring herself to lie.

The thoughts chased around and around in her mind until, exhausted, she fell into dreams as unsettling as her waking life.

Then screams punctured the night.

Carolyn sat up and reached for the light on the table beside her bed. Her fingers found nothing. No lamp. No nightstand. Nothing.

Another shriek jerked her to her feet. She wasn't in her comfortable bedroom. She was sleeping in a horse stall, and the gray fingers of dawn were slipping past the feed sacks covering the windows on the other side of the building.

And a child was terrified.

Grabbing the robe she'd found in the piles of donated clothing, she forced her arms through the floppy sleeves. She rushed to the neighboring stall. Drowsy questions from the others in the stable were fired in her direction, but she paid them no mind. Her toe rammed something on the floor. Tears erupted into her eyes. She half hopped, half ran to the cots where Kevin and Rose Anne slept.

Light flashed from behind her, and she glanced over her shoulder. A shadowed form hung a lantern on a brad by the door. Nodding her thanks, though she couldn't see who'd left it there, she dropped to kneel next to Kevin's cot.

He screeched at the top of his lungs. He thrashed his arms from side to side. His eyes were closed, and she realized he was asleep. On the cot beside his, Rose Anne began to cry in sympathy.

Hoping she was doing the right thing, she soothed her niece as she put her hand on her nephew's shoulder to keep him from throwing himself off the narrow cot. She didn't call his name or wake him. Instead, she protected him from his own panic.

Slowly, he calmed. When he was nestled again into his pillow, she adjusted the blankets twisted around him. She didn't want him to fall out of bed when he tried to loosen them.

She looked at the other cot. Rose Anne had her thumb in her mouth, a sure sign she was distressed, too. She'd stopped sucking her thumb three years ago, but Carolyn had noticed her doing it since the flood. Again she figured the best thing to do was not to mention it and pray the little girl's anxiety would dissipate as their lives returned to normal.

"You need to get back to sleep," Carolyn whispered, smoothing her niece's blanket, too.

"Is something wrong with Kevin?" the little girl whispered.

"Of course not."

"He was yawling, and I was ascared."

Translating Rose Anne's words, she knew the child meant her brother had been yelling and she'd been frightened. Carolyn bent and kissed her on the forehead.

"You don't have to be afraid," Carolyn murmured. "God is always watching over you, and I'm close by if you need me."

"But Kevin is ascared."

"He was having a bad dream."

The little girl shook her head. "It wasn't a bad dream. It was the rain."

"Rain?"

Rose Anne pointed at the roof. "Rain. Lots of it."

It *was* raining, Carolyn realized. Lost in her terror

for Kevin and how he might end up hurting himself, she hadn't noticed rain hammering on the roof.

"We're safe here, sweetheart," she whispered. "You need to go to sleep so you can have fun with Taylor tomorrow."

Kevin sat as she stood. He was wide-awake, and he had his blanket in a white-knuckled grip. "Are we having another hurricane?"

"No, it's just rain." She laughed when thunder boomed in the distance. "A thunderstorm."

"Will we be okay?"

"We'll be fine." She hoped he couldn't see the tears filling her eyes as she wished for a way to banish his memories of the flood. It was impossible, she knew, but that didn't keep her from wanting to spare him more pain.

"Do we need to run away like we did last time?"

She shook her head. "We're safe here." Looking from him to his sister, she added, "The flood never reached here."

"But if it keeps raining—"

"It's going to be okay." She held out her other arm and gathered Rose Anne to her as soon as the little girl had clambered onto the cot. "God is watching over us."

"You said he was watching over us before, but our house is gone."

Tilting Kevin's face toward hers, she said, "Yes, the house is gone, but we're not. God kept us safe because He loves us and we love Him."

"But he didn't save Tip—Tip—Tippy." The child's voice cracked on the name of his stuffed dog that had vanished along with everything else in their house.

And Carolyn's heart broke anew. She'd prayed that somehow, someone sometime would return Tippy to

Kevin. Knowing how much she was asking when God had already let them escape the floodwaters, she couldn't silence the prayer from the center of her soul.

She persuaded the children to go back to sleep. She turned to reach for the lantern. She wanted to take it down and extinguish the flame so the others could find another hour of sleep, as well.

Her fingers halted in midair as she saw Michael standing on the other side of the stall door. He took them as he held his own finger to his lips. Drawing her out of the stall, he closed the door and lifted the lantern off the nail. He said nothing as he led her toward the tack room. He set the lantern on a shelf by the door. Lifting the glass chimney, he blew out the flame.

"What are you doing here at this hour?" Carolyn glanced at the window, which was streaked with thick rivers of rain. "And in this weather?"

"I couldn't sleep." He gave her a smile that she could barely discern in the twilight. "And it wasn't raining when I came out. The clouds opened up as I was passing by, so I ducked inside. I was going to wait out the storm, but then I heard Kevin."

"Why were you walking past the stables this early?"

"I try to walk in a different direction each morning while I spend time talking to God about what I can do that day to help. It was by chance I came up the hill this morning rather than down."

Lightning flashed, followed by thunder. The rattle of hail struck the window, and she flinched in spite of herself.

She forced a smile. "I'd say you made a good decision."

"Or God is trying to tell me something." When another

clap of thunder shook the building, he added, "Though He doesn't need to be so loud. I didn't realize this was where you and the *kinder* were sleeping."

"We're thankful for a warm, dry place to stay."

"Warm?" He glanced around the stables, though she was unsure what he thought he could see in the dim light. "It's going to be cold here when winter comes."

"All the more reason for you to get my house done." She'd meant her words as a joke, but they fell flat when he didn't laugh.

Concern filled his voice. "Are the *kinder* okay?"

"Yes, they'll be fine." Uncomfortable with his small intrusion into her family, she said, "Kevin had a bad dream and woke us up."

"Because of the rain?"

She wanted to say that was silly, but glad she could be honest with him, she said, "It's possible."

"Rebuilding a structure is easy. Rebuilding one's sense of security isn't."

"That sounds like the voice of experience."

He sighed. "My parents died when I was young, and both my twin brother and I had to learn not to expect something horrible was going to happen without warning."

"I'm sorry." She sat on a small stool. "I should have asked more about you and the other volunteers. I've been wrapped up in my own tragedy."

Squatting in front of her so their eyes were even, he said, "At times like this, nobody expects you to be thinking of anything but getting a roof over your *kinder*'s heads."

He didn't reach out to touch her, but she was aware of every inch of him so close to her. His quiet strength had awed her from the beginning. As she'd come to know him better, his fundamental decency had impressed her more. He was a man she believed she could trust.

She shoved that thought aside. Trusting any man would be the worst thing she could do after seeing what *Mamm* had endured during her marriage and then struggling to help Regina escape her abusive husband.

When Carolyn stood, wanting to put some space between herself and this man who could convince her to be as credulous, Michael took a couple of steps back to allow her room. She bit back her yearning to apologize because, if she did, he might ask her to explain. She couldn't. That would reveal too much of her past.

"I'm glad you understand why I must focus on rebuilding a life for the children." The simple statement left no room for misinterpretation. "The flood will always be a part of us, but I want to help them learn how to live with their memories."

He stood, but didn't move closer. "I can't imagine what it was like."

"I can't forget what it was like." She edged toward the window. The rain hid any view of the brook.

"Tell me about it." His voice was soft and invited her to share her burdens with him. Oh, how she wished she could!

"It was loud," she said, choosing each word with care. "Very loud."

"The rush of the water?"

"You've seen the massive boulders along the banks. Those were tumbling into each other, though we didn't know what the terrible noise was at the time. They sounded like cars crashing into each other at a high speed, but the worst was hearing the house struggling to stay on its foundation. As I rushed the children down the stairs and outside, I could hear nails fighting not to be ripped out of the boards holding the house together."

She shuddered and wrapped her arms around herself, wishing the conversation hadn't taken this direction. Most of the time, she could keep those memories at bay by concentrating on getting through the day. So many things required her attention that time rushed by until she could fall into her cot each night.

"Were there people to assist you when you got outside?"

She shook her head. "I sent the kids running up the hill while I made sure the chicken coop was open. I didn't want our chickens to drown, either. I reached Kevin and Rose Anne before they got to the road. It's a good thing, because water was rushing along the road, too, and already washing over both sides. I helped the children get across and we kept going. All I could think about was getting to higher ground where the flood wouldn't reach us."

"And you succeeded."

"I stopped when their little legs couldn't go any farther. We sat on a log and tried to catch our breaths. Then we heard screams for help." She closed her eyes, but forced them open as the appalling scenes burst onto her eyelids like a horror film. "People were trapped in their houses because the water had risen so fast their yards were flooded before they realized what was going on."

"But nobody died in Evergreen Corners."

"I thank God for that with every breath I take, and I thank Him for the courage of our neighbors. Several people with four-wheel-drive pickups backed down as close as they dared through the rising water and threw ropes to those who were trapped. At least one had water seeping into the bed of their truck by the time they'd pulled the last person to safety."

"No wonder Kevin was frightened by the sound of rain tonight."

"The children didn't see any of that. I'd taken them to a shelter set up at the school and left them with Jenna who'd fled the library, bringing some of the irreplaceable books and the patrons who'd been there when water began pouring into the basement."

He shook his head. "I keep hearing stories of narrow escapes, and I try not to imagine how many more there were along the brook."

"Not just this one, but every stream and river in this watershed flooded that night." She started to add more, but halted when a soft cry came from the stall where the children slept.

As she excused herself to go and check on them, she could see the pity on Michael's face. She rushed to calm Rose Anne, who was curled into a sobbing bundle on her cot.

Normally, she would have been bothered by someone having sympathy for her, but if pitying her kept Michael from looking at her with his brown puppy-dog eyes that urged her to trust him, she'd accept it. She couldn't trust any man, because she wouldn't let the children spend their lives witnessing what she had.

Chapter Six

Carolyn yawned as she got dressed. All of them were exhausted. She helped Rose Anne deal with her frustration by pretending to be as incapable as the child at closing the buttons on the little girl's coat. It didn't take much acting because she felt as if her hands were encased in inflexible gloves and her feet in leaden boots.

In only twice as much time as it should have taken, she had the children ready to leave for the day. Rose Anne paused to kiss her stuffed rabbit, Hopper. Wanting to hug Kevin when she saw his devastated expression, Carolyn refrained when he edged away from her. How she wished he would grieve outwardly over losing his cherished stuffed friend! She didn't like how he continued to hold in his sorrow. She knew how caustic unhappiness could be.

She herded the youngsters out. She should be grateful they had a place to stay—and she was!—but she longed for a home where she didn't have to worry about Kevin's night terrors waking others. She would be able to concentrate on helping him. In addition, she longed for a bathroom she could share only with Rose Anne and Kevin.

She was tired of brushing her teeth with water from a galvanized bucket and taking showers where hot water was a rare luxury. The idea of a bath where she could soak until her fingertips were wizened was almost beyond her imagination at this point.

The morning's chill caught her by surprise. She should have expected the weather to change after the thunderstorm. Temperatures were capricious in autumn, jumping from summer to fall to winter in the space of a single day.

"What's going on?" Kevin asked, his sorrow pushed aside as he pointed at where a dozen people were gathering between the library and the seafood restaurant.

"I don't know." She squinted through the dim morning light that burned in her sleep-deprived eyes. Gray clouds lingered over the mountains to the west, obscuring their tops in off-white fuzz.

"Let's go see!" He didn't wait for her answer as he pelted down the hill with Rose Anne on his heels.

Though she'd never felt less like running, especially on grass slick with rain, Carolyn gave chase. The rumble of voices got louder as she drew even with the children. She took them by the hand, but continued on, drawn to the crowd by the undeniable anxiety wafting off the group.

Had something else gone wrong?

She couldn't see over the taller people. For a second, she considered putting Rose Anne on her shoulders and asking the child to give her a report. She almost laughed at the idea of what the child would tell her and how little it might have to do with reality.

Seeing Michael with his friends and several other Amish men, she walked toward where he stood. Kevin yanked his hand out of hers and ran forward to greet Michael with enthusiasm.

Michael looked over her nephew's head and gave her a smile that threatened to melt her knees. He'd been so kind to her this morning, letting her go on and on about the flood. Every instinct urged her to believe he was a good man, and she wanted to listen to her gut. It'd never steered her wrong.

Always a first time, her most sensible mind warned as another part whispered, *Oh, ye of little faith, trust in the Lord with all your heart.*

To hide her uneasy thoughts, Carolyn asked, "What's going on?"

"The road washed out last night." He pointed north, then when she stood on tiptoe to try to see what he was indicating, he drew her forward.

She gasped when she saw the rubble lying next to the only bridge still spanning the brook. The bridge remained sturdy, but the rain had undermined the road. It had collapsed, leaving a band of asphalt not much wider than a railroad track.

"At least…" she began, then halted as the rest of the asphalt caved in and slid down into the brook. The bridge's deck ended in midair on the side closer to her. There was a gap of about six feet between it where the road was gone.

"That does it," said one of the Amish men whose name she couldn't remember. "We're cut off from the outside world until the road across the bridge can be rebuilt."

She resisted her longing to shout her gratitude to God. The people around her wouldn't understand why she was relieved. She'd happily accept being separated from everyone else if it meant Leland couldn't get to town.

"That section of road was weak," someone said behind her. "I'm surprised it hadn't fallen in already."

There was a chorus of agreement, but silence clamped on them at the distant rumble of a truck's engine. Michael and two other men raced toward the abutment. Carolyn watched as the men laced their fingers together and Michael put his foot on them. They raised Michael high enough to grab the top of the abutment with both hands. He scrambled onto the bridge like Kevin used to climb onto the roof of their chicken coop. Running to the far side, he waved his arms to get the driver's attention before the truck reached the bridge.

Carolyn breathed a grateful prayer as the vehicle slowed. She drew the children back as other men rushed past to collect ladders from the general store. In quick order, they were leaned against the abutment, and more men climbed onto the bridge, carrying pieces of wood and tools.

Michael finished talking to the driver before stepping aside to let others erect a temporary barrier by the bridge. Orange barrels left along the side of the road were dragged onto the center line.

Mayor Whittaker walked by with her cell phone close to her ear. She wore a bathrobe under her winter coat and had curlers in her hair. "Now! We need warning signs so nobody drives onto the bridge when the road on one side has collapsed."

"Not safe?" cried Rose Anne. "What about Michael?" She ran toward the abutment.

The mayor lowered her phone and stepped forward to block the little girl. Bending toward her, she said something too low for Carolyn to hear.

Rose Anne whirled and called back, "It's okay as long as Michael isn't in an a-tween wheeler."

"She means an eighteen wheeler," Carolyn translated

in case the mayor was bewildered by Rose Anne's response.

Nodding, Gladys Whittaker put her phone back to her ear and continued to demand what she believed her village needed.

Motioning for Rose Anne to come back to where she and Kevin stood, Carolyn frowned. Kevin was watching the bridge, mesmerized by the sight of the men walking along it. She wanted to warn him not to scale it, but decided she shouldn't give him any ideas. She'd talk to him later when the lure of ladders and an empty bridge wasn't right in front of him.

Benjamin lifted Rose Anne and carried her to Carolyn. The little girl giggled as he blew a loud, buzzing kiss on her cheek.

"*Gute mariye*, Carolyn," he said with a smile as he set her niece on her feet. "Have you met everyone here? If not, let me introduce you while we wait for our hero to return." He winked. "You know James, and the other three are his older brothers. Mathias, Enos and Orris. They've been working on the Gagnon house next door to yours."

The men nodded in her direction, but turned back to talk to James. No, not talk to him, but harangue him, she realized.

She tried not to listen. It wasn't easy to hear his older brothers tell him what he was doing wrong. Or what *they* thought he was doing wrong. They spoke in English. Why? Were they determined that everyone understood what they were saying about James? The list of their beefs with him ran from big to minuscule. It didn't seem to matter to them that he wasn't in charge of arranging which house would receive their delivery of concrete first or that the slight changes in his clothing had been made to comply with the *Ordnung* in the new settlement on Harmony Creek. They acted as if James's sole intention had been to annoy them.

"Don't," Michael said, startling her because she hadn't heard him return.

She hadn't thought she'd ever be unaware of him, and she realized how nettled she was by James's brothers' litany of complaints. "Don't?"

"Don't interfere. I understand that you think it's unfair for them to treat him as they do. I got involved when they first came to Harmony Creek Hollow and acted as if James didn't have a single thought between his ears. He asked me to let him handle it."

"You call that handling it?" She flung out a hand toward the four men. "When Kevin starts to get all bossy, I step in."

"But Kevin is a *kind.* Those are grown men."

"So they should know better."

"I agree, but I also agree with James. It's his problem to handle."

Carolyn had to accede, though she didn't want to. Taking her niece and nephew by the hand again, she left, though every particle of her wanted to announce to James's brothers that they should treasure the time they had with him instead of ruining it with accusations. If she were granted another few minutes with her sister, she wouldn't waste a second of it.

"That was cool!" crowed Kevin to Michael who walked with them. "You kept the truck from falling off the bridge."

"The driver kept it from happening by being quick on his brakes. I just warned him."

Kevin refused to be persuaded. "But you're a hero!"

"God put me and the other men in the right place at the right time."

Seeing how uncomfortable Michael was with Kevin lauding him, Carolyn guessed his unease came from being raised Amish and considering pride a sin. She understood that, but Michael's reluctance seemed to hint there was something more bothering him.

"Are you okay?" she asked beneath the children's excitement.

"I'm fine." He sighed, then smiled faintly. "Sorry, Carolyn. I don't like being ensnared in drama."

"Then you came to the wrong place. Everyone in Evergreen Corners is dripping with drama since the flood." She started to add more, then groaned as the clouds overhead opened like a kitchen faucet.

When he grasped her arm, she let him pull her toward the store. The ground was already soaked, and soil quickly turned to mud. Others were already huddling beneath the wide roof of the wraparound porch. He helped her onto the warped boards, and she was relieved when her boots weren't left behind in the mire. He hefted the children up before jumping out of the storm himself.

She moved closer to the store's wall, hoping to escape the spray from the deluge. A shiver ran an icy finger down her back while she looked at where the wooden steps had been. They'd vanished down the brook. Where had they ended up?

She almost laughed. How would anyone ever be able to differentiate one shattered board from another? Paint had been stripped off by the gravel swept along in the water. It had raised the brook's bed almost two inches. Dredging had begun farther upstream, but she had no idea when the equipment would get to Evergreen Corners.

Especially now that the last bridge was unusable while the road was out.

Michael leaned his right shoulder against the wall, so he faced her. When she looked at him, she was astounded by how close his face was to hers. She lowered her eyes and turned away.

What was wrong with her? She shouldn't be imagining how his lips would feel against hers. She'd promised herself—and God—that she would learn the lessons He'd placed before her when she witnessed *Mamm* and her sister with abusive husbands. She couldn't risk making the same error, not when the children depended on her.

"You aren't dramatic, Carolyn," Michael murmured. When she raised her eyes to meet his steady gaze, he said, "You can't know how much I admire how you stay calm in the middle of the biggest tempest." He shook his head as the rain seemed to fall harder. "Maybe we should stop saying words like *tempest*, *drip* or *pour*."

"Now who's being dramatic?"

She meant her question as a joke to defuse the tension hardening his shoulders into a taut line. When he recoiled from her words, she was shocked.

Though she wanted to ask him why he was leery of what he called drama, Carolyn simply said, "It shouldn't take them long to fix the road and reconnect it to the bridge. It was quick for the roadbed to be rebuilt last time."

"There's more debris and rocks to move because the whole section collapsed." He gave her a wry grin. "Or at least that's what I was told. I know exactly nothing about building roads."

"We're all learning a lot about things we never thought we'd ever need to know."

He didn't answer as Glen stepped onto the porch with one easy motion. Shaking rain off his baseball cap, the project director said, "Not how I planned to start the day."

"Do we have enough supplies for today?" Michael asked.

"I've got a 4x4 truck if someone needs it." Glen tapped his forefinger against his cheek. "We've been keeping it for when someone needs to travel north because that road out of town has been iffy since the flood. Some of the locals cut a route through the woods behind the diner to reach Ludlow."

Carolyn wasn't the only one on the porch who sighed at the mention of the diner that had been a popular meeting place. Whole sections of the building were gone, but the owner had vowed to rebuild. She hoped he would be interested in buying her baked goods again. A large portion of her income before the flood had been from providing pies and cakes and cookies to the diner. Now she was dependent on her neighbors and groups like the Amish Helping Hands to provide food and shelter for her and the children.

When Glen spoke her name, she focused on the project director again as he said, "We'll be ready later today to begin excavating the new cellar for your house, Carolyn, and we've got plenty of diesel. Of course, we need it to stop raining."

As he spoke, the storm stopped. Everybody laughed at the coincidence.

Carolyn gathered the children because they were late for breakfast. She went with them, though she wished she could have stayed on the porch with Michael until he explained what had dimmed his eyes when he spoke about drama. He was doing so much to help her. It seemed

only right she should offer him an ear if he wanted to
unburden himself.

Or her lips for a kiss.

Michael stepped back from the cellar hole and tested
aching muscles that had been challenged that day. Rebuilding the road had taken almost three days, using ma-
chinery brought in for excavating the cellars. The state's
equipment had been allocated elsewhere. Glen and his
volunteers had assisted the town crew in reconnecting the
bridge to the single lane road running through the center
of Evergreen Corners. It was only a temporary fix, but it
kept supplies moving into town and let concrete trucks
deliver their loads.

He couldn't remember the last time he'd done masonry
work, and he remembered why he'd avoided it. Cement
wasn't like wood, beautiful and intriguing to the touch.
The concrete forms outlining the new dimensions of the
house had to be level in every direction. Unlike the old
cellar, which had been plowed in before they'd begun
work on the new foundation, the new cellar hole needed
to be waterproof. The old cellar walls had been layers of
stone with dirt between them.

He eyed the new foundation. He'd seen Isaac measuring each corner to make sure it was as close to ninety de-
grees as possible. The newcomer had insisted on making
changes to the wall facing the brook because he hadn't
been satisfied with the line Michael and James set in
place. Though the work of pulling up the stakes and reset-
ting them had been tedious, Michael hadn't complained.
He respected a man who took such care with his work.
Glen had agreed to bring all the volunteers to work on
the Wiebe family's foundation. With the first foundation

poured, they would move to the Gagnons' house next door and then on to the third house. That one would become Rhiannon Cadwallader's home. The widow, whom everyone called Rhee, had been rescued seconds before her house crumbled. She currently lived in the basement of the church where she'd once preached.

After working a couple of days with Isaac Kauffman, Michael had no doubt Glen had decided to give in because Isaac wouldn't. He might be the most stubborn, exacting man Michael had ever met, but he backed his demands with precise work. Michael looked forward to using his own skills when it came to adding molding and cabinets to the house.

Taking a piece of rough board and smoothing it and shaping it seemed to bring him closer to God. When he mitered corners or added stain to bring out the beauty of the grain, his fingers created a hymn of praise to the greatest Maker who'd put the pieces of the world together in perfect order.

He bent and lifted one of the stakes that had been tossed aside because the notch had failed. Turning it in his hands, he pulled out his pocketknife. Four quick strokes cut out a place where the string could be hooked into place. Several had broken while preparing this foundation, so they needed all they had for the next ones.

"Hey, Michael!"

At the shout in a young voice, he looked over his shoulder as Kevin came bounding toward him. Did Carolyn know the boy was here? *Ja*, she was talking to Glen as they bent over a stack of long pages on a large rock. He recognized them as the plans for the new house.

"*Gute mariye*, Kevin," he called back.

"Did you say *good morning*?"

"I did. *Gut* guess."

"That one's easy. They sound a lot alike, and I remember hearing it before." Without a pause, he asked, "What are you doing?"

Michael had to smile. The boy's endless curiosity reminded him of himself at Kevin's age. At first, he'd been given answers. However, as he grew older and learned to read, his adoptive father had provided him with simple books where he could find the answers on his own. The day he'd first entered the public library and discovered the array of resources waiting there had been one of the happiest of his whole life.

Until he met Carolyn and her *kinder* and was able to spend time with them.

He hadn't guessed he'd find youngsters of their ages fascinating. He liked how he never could guess what they'd do or say next.

He showed Kevin the stick and his pocketknife. "I'm making a new stake for the Gagnons' house."

"How?"

Running the knife along the wood, he demonstrated. "It's called whittling."

"Why are you a wit-ling?" asked Rose Anne who'd followed her brother. She peered down into the cellar.

Folding his knife and sticking it in his pocket, Michael swept an arm around her waist. He picked her up so she wouldn't tumble over the edge. Her laugh tickled his heart and made him want to join in. He smiled at Carolyn as she walked toward them.

"She means whittling," Carolyn said.

"I was hoping so, but I guess wit-ling is better than witless." He put Rose Anne down and watched as the two children ran to get a closer look at the bulldozer parked a few feet away. "She knows how to make new words when she doesn't understand something, ain't so?"

"She's trying to keep up with her big brother."

"That sounds like the voice of experience. Did you have a big brother you needed to keep up with, too?"

"No, a big sister." She looked away as if she'd said something she hadn't planned to.

He couldn't guess what it was, but there were many things about Carolyn Wiebe that baffled him.

Deciding the best thing to do was not press her, he said, "What would you think of me teaching Kevin to whittle? He seems interested, and he's about the same age I was when I started."

"Maybe so, but I know how enthusiastic he can get and how he can toss common sense out the window."

"Then we'll work outside."

She frowned at him. He wasn't sure if it was because of his weak jest or because she was upset he joked about something she took seriously.

Holding up his hands, he said, "Just trying to lighten the mood."

"By showing you can be as absurd as Kevin is when he gets overexcited?"

"Ouch." He put his hand to the center of his chest and rocked back several steps.

"Michael!" Exasperation filled her voice.

He relented. "I'm sorry, Carolyn. I know I shouldn't pick on you when it's something you care about as much as you do your *kinder*."

"I don't like the idea of him cutting off a finger or two." A faint smile tilted her lips. "Or you, either."

He wiggled his fingers. "So far, so good, and I've been

whittling since I was five or six. Learning what a stick of wood could become led me to wanting to do more."

"So you became a carpenter. Will you be framing our house?"

"*Ja*, I'll be one of the framers. The work doesn't require much imagination. I like being able to see a piece of wood and figuring out what it could become. A two-by-four is already pretty much all it's going to be." He chuckled. "That's why I'm looking forward more to working on the finish carpentry in your house."

"Me, too, because that will mean the work is almost done, and we can move into a real house again instead of living in two stalls in a stable. I shouldn't complain. After all, a stable was good enough for a very special baby's birth."

"That is very true." He gestured toward the cellar hole. "Do you want to see what we've done? We can start with what Benjamin and I finished." He crooked a finger. "This way."

He walked toward the trees and heard her gasp when she caught sight of the rectangle of chicken wire that made a pen for her vagabond chickens. She ran to it, lacing her fingers through the wire and examining how he and his friends had hooked more wire to the top.

"We didn't want to let your pesky poultry fly out," he said with a chuckle.

"As long as they've got plenty to eat, they're content not to wander." She counted the chickens. "All nine hens are here! You found them all."

"They found us. I think they're happy to be home and safe from predators." He watched her face as she cooed at her beloved hens who came waddling over to her, hoping for more food though corn was scattered on the ground. "And your rooster—an ornery fellow, I've got to say—was captured by a deputy sheriff who took him to a nearby farm. I can find out which one. He's—"

"Doodle."

"I hope that's the name of the rooster and not the deputy."

She laughed, the sound lighter than he'd ever heard from her. "Yes, Doodle is our rooster. I told you the kids chose the chickens' names, though they had help from our friends." She pointed at each of the hens in turn. "There's Henrietta. Henley. Henster is the one at the back. Hendrix and Henmeister. Henna. Little Red Hen and Big Red Hen. And, of course, Henny Penny."

Glad to laugh along with her, he felt a flush of satisfaction—something he hadn't experienced in a while—rush through him as she thanked him for collecting the chickens and building the wire pen. She was more delighted when he told her that he planned to rebuild her coop for her.

"But first," he said, "we've got to get you and the *kinder* into your house. *Komm mol*, and you can have a look down at your new cellar. There's not much to see at this point because it's empty, but I know you'd like to see what progress we've made."

"I don't want to get in the way."

"There's nothing more we can do here until the concrete finishes curing. If we put up walls too soon, we risk damaging the foundation."

"How long will that take?"

"About a week?"

"A week?" The word came out in a squawk.

"Pray for warmer and drier weather because it'll shorten the time, but we want to pour the other two foundations before we start framing your house." He led her to where she could look down into the cellar. "It'll be worth the wait because you won't have water leaking in as you did with your old house."

Her eyes cut toward the sleepy brook, and he wondered if she was reliving how she'd feared for her life and the *kinder*'s. He resisted his yearning to give her a hug as he would have Kevin or Rose Anne. She wasn't a *kind*. She was a beautiful woman shadowed by tragedy.

Ja, she was a lovely woman, and he'd spent too many hours thinking about her and how it would be to hold her close.

But he couldn't. Not until he made his final decision if he'd be baptized or not. The choice must not be influenced by his burgeoning feelings for her, feelings that made his fingers quiver at the thought of touching her.

Chapter Seven

Michael couldn't wait for Carolyn to appear at the neighboring work site four days later while they watched the first concrete truck start pouring its load into the forms for the cellar of the house next door to hers. The news he had for her today should bring one of her gentle smiles. He hoped he wouldn't burst with what he had to share with her.

At last, she arrived. She carried a tray. The cups of *kaffi* on it sent out an inviting aroma that drew the workers toward her like bees to a patch of flowers. Someone grabbed a cup for the guy operating the truck.

As Michael stood to one side to let the others take their cups, there was only one thing more enticing than the *kaffi*'s scent. Carolyn herself. Her blond hair was drawn back at her nape beneath a small round lace *kapp*. Beneath a black apron, her lilac dress was decorated with small flowers in a scattered pattern and accented by her gold locket. The image of a sweet, plain woman was ruined by the heavy work boots someone had given her so she didn't ruin her sneakers in the mud.

"How's it going?" she asked as he took one of the last cups.

"It feels *gut* to be moving forward again."

Michael drained his cup while Carolyn collected empty ones. "Do you have a few minutes?" he asked when she held out the tray to him in a silent invitation to add his cup. "I'd like to talk to you about something important."

"I need to return the tray, and—"

He didn't give her a chance to continue. Putting two fingers in his mouth, he let loose a whistle in the direction of a pair of teens. One *Englisch* boy whose name he thought was Jack turned to look at him. Since work on the Gagnon house had resumed a few days ago, about a half-dozen *Englisch* teens, both boys and girls, had been hanging around after school. They wanted to help, but Glen had been firm that volunteers had to be approved by Amish Helping Hands and the Mennonite project director before they could work.

Michael didn't agree because the teens were as eager as he would have been at their ages to help rebuild their village. Maybe he should mention that to Glen and suggest the teens be found chores at the work sites. He valued Glen's vast experience, but there must be tasks they could ask the kids to do.

Later, he'd make a point of seeking out Glen.

For now, he motioned to the lad he thought was named Jack to come closer. Taking the tray from Carolyn, he handed it to Jack.

"Can you take this to the community center's kitchen?" he asked.

When the boy hesitated, not wanting to miss watching the concrete being poured, Carolyn said, "There are extra cinnamon rolls left over from breakfast. Tell them I said you should get two for bringing back the tray."

"Can we both go?" He pointed toward his friend who'd been listening while trying not to appear to.

Michael glanced at Carolyn and saw her nod. "I'm sure the offer is *gut* for two."

"Thanks!" The kid grabbed the tray and with his friend hurried in the direction of the community center.

"What do you need to talk to me about?" Carolyn asked as another truck reached the site.

So many things, he wanted to reply. He wondered about her life as a conservative Mennonite, and he wondered what had happened to her husband. She never mentioned him. The kids didn't, either, he realized with a bolt of shock. He'd been so involved in the disaster relief work, he hadn't given any thought to Carolyn's husband.

"Michael?" she asked, and he knew he'd been mired in his thoughts too long.

He chided himself for being distracted when at last she was standing beside him and he could share the news he'd been waiting to tell her. Making sure he didn't smile and give away his surprise, he said, "I wanted to let you know you and the *kinder* won't be sleeping in the stables tonight. You're being moved elsewhere."

Puzzlement threaded her brow. "What? Where are we moving to?"

"It's simple." He couldn't halt his grin. "You'll be living in the trailer, and Benjamin, James and I will use the cots in the stable. After all, we're not as susceptible to colds as the *kinder* are."

"You're working hard every day. You need to have somewhere comfortable to sleep."

"We aren't working any harder than you are, and

you're taking care of two active *kinder*, as well." He put his hands on her shoulders and bent so he could look into her eyes. "Most important, Carolyn, there's plenty of insulation in the trailer's roof, and that will deaden the sound of rain."

Her eyes widened, and he found himself wondering if a man could get lost exploring their deep brown depths. He looked away before he ended up gawping at her with the same expression her son had worn when Kevin watched the bulldozer push in the foundation of their old house.

"I didn't think of that," she said.

"Those little ones have endured enough, don't you think?"

"But to put you out of your comfortable beds—"

"Comfortable? Three men in such a tiny space isn't what I'd describe as comfortable." When she opened her mouth to protest further, he held up a single finger. "One thing you should know about plain men, Carolyn. When we set our minds on a course of action to help someone else, nothing deters us."

"You're making that up."

"Maybe. Maybe not." He was relieved to see her resistance to the idea crumbling. "But it doesn't matter. We can move our stuff out and your stuff in while the concrete is being poured. We're in the way here anyhow." He waved to his friends who'd waited near the road.

"I don't know what to say."

"Say thank you."

Her shoulders dropped, and her smile softened. "Thank you. I should—"

"No," Benjamin interjected as he and James joined them. "You shouldn't do anything. Let us take care of it." He grinned at Michael. "So glad you got a chance to tell her what we decided. I hope she didn't object too much to what is common sense."

"Not too much." She smiled.

Did it brighten when she aimed it at him? Michael wanted to think so.

Carolyn had to wonder what others must think when she followed Michael, his two friends and the children she'd collected from the day care center in a bizarre parade.

She wasn't surprised to see Kevin trailing Michael as if he were the man's shadow. Rose Anne was dancing around, almost getting in the way on each step. Nobody seemed to mind as they talked and laughed with her nephew and niece.

This was what she wanted for her sister's children. To have in their lives strong, gentle men who would treat them as special gifts from God. She prayed God had concealed any memories Kevin had of his father and thanked Him that Rose Anne was too young to recall the horrific scenes the children had witnessed.

Kevin stopped to peer into some used cars, and Rose Anne had to be lifted to do the same. He decided Carolyn should replace the sedate black sedan that had washed away in the flood with a bright silver SUV. The children were accustomed to her driving a car, a skill she'd mastered when she decided to live as a Mennonite and another example of how far she'd removed herself from the life she'd assumed she would live as an Amish woman. Telling him she'd keep his suggestion in mind, she convinced the children to keep going.

There were a pair of trailers parked behind the dealership. One was small, shaped like a horizontal teardrop and made to tow behind a car. The other was a much grander vehicle with a steering wheel set behind its large windshield. Double sets of tires front and back were needed for such a big RV. She caught sight of a rectangular bay that stuck out the far side to give more room to the interior.

They went to the smaller trailer. Though Benjamin had made it clear all three men had agreed to switching places, she had no doubts Michael was the catalyst behind the idea. Not that he would admit it. No Amish man would lay claim to such a good idea, because to do so would hint of pride.

James opened the door and stepped back. "Be careful. There are three steps in there."

Carolyn thanked him and lifted Kevin and then Rose Anne onto the steps. Inside, the trailer wasn't much bigger than the two stalls at Mr. Aiken's stables. Looking past the miniature kitchen with its dull green appliances and sink, she saw a bedroom at the back and realized the trailer was the size of three stalls. The extra room would give her privacy she hadn't had since the flood.

She gasped when she saw a stacked washer and dryer in the bedroom. "Do they work?"

"*Ja*, they do now," Michael said, coming up the steps. "We fixed them last week and got them hooked up."

What luxury! Their old house hadn't had a washer or dryer, though she'd seen space for them on the plan in the new house.

In front of her was a narrow sofa with cushions covered in striped fabric the same green as the stove. To her right beneath a low ceiling was a table with a curved bench along the outer wall of the trailer. More cushions matched the ones on the sofa.

She edged out of the way as the other two men entered. With all of them inside, she understood why they'd been eager to swap. There wasn't room for them even if she and the children hadn't been there.

"Sorry about the dirty dishes in the sink," Benjamin said, embarrassed.

"I hardly noticed them," she said as she unbuttoned her coat. The trailer had been toasty warm when she stepped in, and now, with all of them crowded in it, the air was beginning to feel as if she'd crawled into the oven. "This is wonderful."

"I don't know if I'd call it *wunderbaar*." Michael laughed. "But it should be much more comfortable for you and the *kinder*."

His words made her think again of how chilly it would be in the stables as the mercury dropped night after night as winter approached. "I can't ask you to give up—"

Her protest was interrupted when Kevin climbed on the sofa and grabbed the edge of the low ceiling over the table. He hauled himself up, rolled onto his belly and peered over the edge. "Can I sleep here?"

"It's a bunk bed with a single bunk," Michael said when her confusion must have been visible.

"I'll sleep in the corner and won't fall out." Kevin clasped his hands together. "Please! I promise to be careful."

Before she could answer, Michael said in a whisper, "We'll rig up something so he won't fall out. A couple of narrow slats will let him climb in and out, but keep him from rolling over the edge while he's asleep."

"All right, Kevin. You can sleep there after Michael fixes it into a bed."

"It's not a bed?" He looked at them in astonishment.

"There's a mattress. All I need is a pillow and some blankets."

"We used the area for storage," Michael answered.

Undaunted, her nephew asked, "When can you fix it, Michael?"

"Probably this evening. I need to get some supplies, and then once I'm done, you can sleep there every night until your house is finished."

Kevin's eyes filled with abrupt tears. "Tippy would love being here. It's the kind of place he likes."

Michael looked at her, puzzled. "Tippy?"

She blinked back tears of her own. "Tippy is—he was the stuffed dog he'd had since he was a baby."

"Gone?"

She nodded, glad she didn't have to explain more. As she moved to ask Kevin at which end he'd want to put his pillow, in hopes of distracting him from his sorrow, she heard Michael draw in a deep breath and release it through pursed lips. She wanted to remind him that some things were out of their hands and they needed to trust God had a reason for what had happened along Washboard Brook.

But that wasn't easy when one small boy had lost his only connection to Indiana. She knew Kevin didn't think of Tippy like that. Carolyn wasn't sure how much her nephew remembered of his life before they'd come to Evergreen Corners. It was a topic she wouldn't bring up, and he hadn't asked.

Someday she was going to have to be honest with him and with Rose Anne.

Not today.

When Kevin was calmer, she discovered Benjamin and James had slipped out of the trailer. She didn't see them outside, so she wondered if they'd returned to the Gagnons' work site.

Rose Anne tugged on Michael's pants leg. "What about me?"

"We've got a special place for you. Watch." Michael bent over the sofa built against the wall. When he pulled on the seat cushion, the base rolled out enough to let the cushion on the back fall into place to make a twin bed.

The little girl clapped her hands with glee before climbing onto the cushions and lying down. "My own real live growed-up bed."

Again Carolyn had to blink back tears. They filled her eyes each time one of the children mentioned how they'd been roughing it. How she wished they'd never had to experience losing everything and living in the stable!

Now…

She put her hand on Michael's strong arm and whispered, "Thank you."

"It's nothing."

"No, it's the answer to a prayer." She glanced at where Rose Anne was standing on her bed and peeking into the space where Kevin would sleep. "You've made the children so happy."

"And you?"

"You've made me happy, too." Heat rose up her cheeks, and she guessed she was blushing. "Thank you, Michael."

"I'm glad to be able to help. I know Benjamin and James are, too."

Was that his way of severing the sudden connection between them? If so, she should be grateful because her fingers tingled with a longing to lace them through his as she stepped closer to him. She couldn't do that. Until she knew the children were safe from Leland, she must avoid getting their lives involved with anyone else's.

"Please thank them for us." She edged away. "No, don't do that. Instead, ask them to come here tomorrow night after supper. I'd like to try out this oven and bake a cake."

"Cake?" cried the children as one. "Yummy!"

"How can I resist such an invitation?" asked Michael, his eyes twinkling. "After all I've heard about your baking, we'll be excited to sample it."

"Good. Come tomorrow night after supper."

"We'll have time before tomorrow evening's planning meeting." He winked at the children. "And if we're a little late, it'll be worth it, ain't that so?"

"Mommy makes the bestest cakes in the whole big, wide world," Rose Anne said, crossing her arms over her narrow chest as if daring someone to challenge her assertion. "The *gut-est*, right, Michael?"

Carolyn fought her smile. "Rose Anne, we shouldn't brag about the gifts God has given to us."

"Even when it's the truth?"

Putting her arm around the little girl, Carolyn sat beside her on the extended sofa. "Whether it's the truth or not, it's not something we brag about to the world. We should—"

"Let everyone find out for themselves," said Kevin, looking over the edge.

Rose Anne nodded. "And then everyone will find out Mommy's cakes are the bestest things in the whole wide world."

Giving her niece a hug, she said, "No, you are the bestest thing in the whole wide world." She smiled at

Kevin. "Both of you are the bestest things in the whole wide world."

"You can't have two bestest things," he argued.

"Maybe not, but you two are the bestest things in my world."

Her answer set both children to laughing. When a deeper chuckle rumbled underneath their voices, she couldn't help her gaze from rising to meet Michael's.

His warm eyes twinkled as the skin around them crinkled to reveal lines left by frequent good humor. "And if you're wondering, we haven't forgotten about you." He gestured toward the other end of the trailer. "There's a real bed in the bedroom. Not as interesting as the two out here, but it'll give you more privacy than you've had."

"How can we thank you for all you've done for us?"

"The cake will be a *gut* place to start." His easy grin sent a sweet warmth uncurling through her middle.

For the first time, she didn't try to dampen it. Instead, she wanted to savor the luscious sensation while he explained to her that once they had the men's clothing and supplies out of the trailer, he'd help her and the children move their things from the stable. She looked forward to spending the rest of the morning with him.

Enjoying their time together wouldn't last forever, so she intended to appreciate every second now.

Chapter Eight

Eager to discuss his ideas with Glen about putting the village teenagers to work, Michael headed toward the project director's office at the high school the next morning. He undid his coat, glad for the warmth billowing along the empty hallway. Carolyn hadn't been kidding when she said the trailer was more comfortable than the stables. Though the building was heated, the system was meant for horses, not humans. A chill had fallen on everything by morning, making his blanket feel as if it'd been left outside.

On the other hand, he hadn't bumped elbows with James and Benjamin while they got ready for the day. Shaving with the small mirror he'd brought from the trailer and using a water bucket had been simpler than standing at the teeny kitchen sink.

When Michael reached the classroom Glen had taken over as his office, he peered through the big glass window in the door. The scholars' desks had been removed, leaving marks on the parquet flooring. In addition to the teacher's desk, a half dozen folding tables had been brought in for the project director's use. A blackboard held a schedule with each volunteer's name listed under the projects for the three houses. A schedule had been sketched in, though the board showed plenty of erasures.

From another wing of the building, he could hear voices. The students must be arriving for the day. Aromas announced the cafeteria staff was already at work and *kaffi* was brewing in the teachers' lounge.

Michael knocked on the door and nodded when Glen motioned for him to enter. Every flat surface was covered with papers and books and file folders in a variety of colors. Two whiteboards with black markers sitting in the trays at the bottom displayed more lists. Supplies on order, Michael guessed after a quick glance, and delivery dates.

What a task to keep the projects on track with both supplies and workers! Glen must have more patience than Michael ever would have, as well as an ability to see both the big picture for the projects and the tiniest details.

"What brings you here today?" Glen asked, picking up a cup. He took a sip, then grimaced. "This coffee wasn't good when it was fresh. It's gone downhill since."

"I'll bring you some *gut kaffi* from the community center on my way to the work site."

Glen smiled. "A debt I may never be able to repay. This stuff is going to rot my taste buds and my stomach."

"How about repaying that debt by listening to an idea I've got?"

"Ideas can't repay a debt, especially if they're good ones." Motioning for Michael to get one of the folding chairs stored in a corner, he asked, "What's on your mind?"

Michael didn't bother to sit as he spoke about finding work in the afternoon for the teens who were interested in becoming a part of the rebuilding. Leaning his hands on the edge of the desk, he said, "I think it'd be worthwhile for you to arrange for the teenagers, who've been hanging around the job sites, to help."

"We can't be responsible for minors, and getting signed permission from their parents will take time away from other work we need to do." Glen glanced out the windows at the low, gray sky that warned of a mid-November snowstorm. "No matter how much we want to ignore the fact, winter will be here before we know it."

"I'm not talking about them doing construction work. What they could do is be available at each site to run errands so we won't have to spend valuable time chasing down tools or something to drink. I would trust Kevin to do something this simple, so it shouldn't be a problem for teenagers."

Glen leaned back in his chair, folded his hands over his chest and considered the idea. "Y'know, Michael, that's an excellent idea. I must admit asking teens to be errand boys—"

"And girls."

He chuckled. "Errand boys and girls. Usually, when we get involved in such projects, the teens are busy with school and their own lives and don't have time to volunteer."

"They seem eager to help, and we could use the extra hands."

"I agree one hundred percent." Glen closed his eyes and rubbed his forehead before folding his arms on the papers spread across the table. "Let me talk to Mayor Whittaker. If she's okay with it, let's give it a trial run."

Pushing back from the desk, Michael said, "*Gut.*

That's all I have. Anything you want me to share with my team?"

"I hear you, James and Benjamin traded your sleeping quarters."

"That's right. Should we have cleared it with you first?"

Glen waved a hand in his direction. "Of course not, but keep me informed. Okay? If someone needs a list of where our volunteers are, I need to be able to provide it right away."

"Who would need such a list?"

"Someone with too much time on their hands. Nothing we'd know anything about."

"True." He turned to leave, but paused when Glen called his name.

"Well done, by the way," the project director said with a smile.

"The forms for the concrete—"

"I'm not talking about that. I'm talking about you guys offering your cushy quarters to Carolyn and her kids. That was decent of you."

"It seemed like the right thing to do."

"It was." Glen's jaw worked before he said, "If it's none of my business, tell me so, but is there something going on between you and Carolyn?"

Michael knew he couldn't hesitate. Nor could he lie. "I'm Amish, and she's not."

"Things aren't that simple."

"It is for me." Again that was the truth, though he wasn't going to divulge that. Until he knew what he wanted his future to be, he must not let his heart get involved with any woman beyond casual friendship.

Too bad his heart didn't want to agree.

* * *

It wasn't her home, but putting a bowl of steaming vegetables on the small table at the front of the trailer made Carolyn feel more at home than she had in almost a month. She opened the oven and checked the chicken and noodles casserole was browning properly.

"When do we eat?" asked Rose Anne from the sofa where she played with a doll someone had given her.

Unlike the faceless rag dolls Carolyn had as a child, this one had molded features. Its bright purple hair clashed with an outfit of every color in the rainbow. Carolyn's dolls had had sedate plain clothes like the ones she'd worn. They'd had bare feet instead of what looked like a cross between sneakers and a truncated skateboard. But Rose Anne loved the silly doll, and having her happy was what was important now.

"Not until Michael gets here," called Kevin from by the door. "Shouldn't he be here by now?"

"Michael and his friends will get here when they're done with work and have had a chance to clean up." She wagged a finger at the children. "Something you need to do. Go and wash your hands and faces. With soap this time."

Ignoring their grumbling, Carolyn kept her smile hidden until Kevin and Rose Anne somehow squeezed into the minuscule bathroom together. She listened for giggling, a sure sign of mischief, as she opened up the fridge and took out apple butter to serve with the biscuits she'd made earlier. She hoped they were edible because the gauge on the front of the oven seemed to have little to do with the actual temperature inside it.

At a knock on the door, she wiped her hands on a towel

and reached to open it. Michael stepped into the trailer, the hair along his face still damp.

"It's cold out there," he said with a big shudder, "but it smells *wunderbaar* in here."

"Take off your coat and sit while I finish." She barely got the words out before the children ran from the bathroom, their hands dripping, to greet him.

Reaching over their heads, she took his coat and hung it in the closet by the bedroom door. There was plenty of room with the few pieces of clothing the kids had. She closed the door and watched Michael listen as Rose Anne introduced him to the garish doll she'd named Brie.

"Like the cheese?" he asked.

"No, like Taylor."

Carolyn stepped forward to say, "Taylor is Rose Anne's best friend, and Taylor's middle name is Brie."

"Ah," he replied, standing straighter so his head almost touched the ceiling, "now I understand."

"Where are James and Benjamin?"

"James's older brothers decided he needed to spend time with them tonight, and Benjamin raised his hand when your village librarian—"

"Jenna."

"That's it. Jenna was looking for volunteers to help carry ruined books out of the building. Apparently she's been stashing some of the older, valuable books in freezers throughout the village in the hope of saving them."

She nodded, though she saw the truth in his eyes. He believed his friends had come up with excuses to allow him to spend time with her and her family. She should be bothered Benjamin and James had made such an assumption, but she couldn't be. The idea of spending the evening with Michael was delightful.

Telling the others to sit so she could get the casserole out of the oven without the risk of burning anyone, she listened as Kevin and Rose Anne chattered. They were eager to share every facet of their day, down to the smallest details of how one of the other children had spilled his juice at lunch. Twice.

When she placed the casserole on a folded towel in the center of the table, she set a ladle next to it. She went to the refrigerator and got out the small carton of milk. There wasn't room for the gallon jug she usually bought. Setting it on the table, she filled two glasses with water for herself and Michael.

"There's not enough milk for—" she began.

He halted her by raising his hand. "You don't have to explain or apologize, Carolyn. Don't forget. I know the challenges of living in this soup can."

That set the children to giggling again.

Carolyn sat across the table from Michael with Kevin next to him and Rose Anne beside her. When her knee brushed his as she stretched to push her nephew's hair back out of his eyes, heat rose through her. She guessed her cheeks were the color of the bright red bow on Rose Anne's doll.

He shifted to give her room and acted as if he hadn't seen her blush. "Shall we thank God for our supper?"

"I'll say grace!" announced Kevin, raising his hand as if in school.

Carolyn glanced at Michael. Before a meal, the Amish didn't give thanks aloud, but each person prayed in silence to God in their own words. He caught her eyes and nodded he was fine with Kevin saying grace. She tensed, wondering if she'd betrayed the truth. She let her shoulders droop when she remembered how many breakfasts he'd taken with the other volunteers. She could have observed their heads bowed in silence at any one of them.

Kevin rushed through grace so quickly she doubted she would have understood a single word if they didn't say the same prayer each night. A grin tugged at Michael's expressive mouth, but he said at the end along with her and Rose Anne, "Amen."

"You can say grace next time, Michael," Kevin said with a big grin.

"Maybe you'd like to see how the Amish pray." Michael folded his arms on the table. "We've got a church Sunday this weekend. You're welcome to attend if you'd like."

Carolyn gasped, astonished by his invitation to someone he saw as *Englisch*.

"The service is three hours or so long," he went on when she didn't reply. "We have a communal meal afterward, and the *kinder* always spend the afternoon playing games while the rest of us enjoy the news of the past two weeks."

"Can we go?" Rose Anne asked, bouncing in her seat.

"I want to go!" Kevin never was subtle about his feelings.

"It's not for *kinder* to make these decisions." Michael's gentle scold had an instant effect on her niece and nephew as they quieted and looked at her.

She knew so many reasons she should decline, but heard herself agreeing to go. One day, when she could reveal the truth to the children, they would have a memory of how Amish spent a church Sunday. It might make it easier for them to decide what sort of life they wanted.

Not wanting to discuss the topic any longer, because she must avoid any suggestion that she knew more about an Amish worship service than an *Englischer* should, she tucked a napkin in the neck of Rose Anne's dress. "I hope you're hungry. I made enough for us and James and Benjamin."

"As *gut* as it smells, they're going to be sorry they didn't come." Michael leaned forward toward the casserole. "I see you made wedding chicken." He laughed when the kids stared at him, wide-eyed. "Chicken and noodles are one of the main dishes we serve at weddings."

"But nobody's getting merry," Rose Anne lamented. "No chicken for us?"

Carolyn smiled as Michael scooped out a ladle of the casserole and put it on her niece's plate.

"We'll pretend someone got *merry*," he said with a quick grin in Carolyn's direction. "That way, we can eat as if we're at a wedding party."

And it was a party as they sat at the cramped table in the tiny trailer and ate and laughed. For the first time in longer than she could remember, Carolyn felt as if she could set her burdens of worry and fear aside for the evening. The children were as carefree. Michael had given them a wondrous gift that night.

Chapter Nine

On Sunday morning, with the sun a finger's width over the horizon and a blustery wind battering the trailer, Carolyn heard from the upper bunk in the trailer, "Is today the day?"

Kevin spent most of his time when they were inside up there. Sometimes with his sister, other times on his own. The bunk had become a variety of imaginary places in the past week for her niece and nephew. Last night, it'd been a rocket to the moon. The children had imagined it was a train earlier in the afternoon.

Carolyn paused in folding the blankets that had been tucked around Rose Anne overnight. Looking at where the boy was buttoning his shirt, she asked, "Is today the day for what?"

"Is today the day I should pray Tippy will be found?"

"Kevin…"

He turned away, hearing her hesitation as she struggled to find something to say.

"Kevin," she repeated. "Please listen to me."

He looked over his shoulder.

She clutched the blanket, wishing she could swaddle

him in it and keep all his sorrows at bay. "Every day is a good day to pray. God doesn't get tired of hearing what's in our hearts."

"So if I pray, He'll listen?"

"He'll listen, and he'll answer in His time and in His own way. We have to trust He knows what's best for us, even if it's not always the answer we want to hear."

"You mean, He may not find Tippy for me."

"I don't know." She held his gaze. "Only God knows what's to come. All He asks of us is to have faith in Him."

He considered that, then nodded. She waited for him to ask another question, but he began talking with his sister about the Amish church service.

When Carolyn opened the closet to take out their coats and hats, she caught sight of her own reflection in the full-length mirror hanging inside the door. She hoped God understood why she wasn't wearing the *kapp* she used to wear and why her polyester dress was a bright blue. She shut the door, but couldn't silence her misgivings at how her life had been altered by the man who'd abused her sister and threatened his own children.

It wasn't just the cold morning that sent Carolyn hurrying with Kevin and Rose Anne across the village green. Until Michael invited her to attend the Amish service, she hadn't realized how much she'd missed participating in what had once been normal. The children were curious but a little bit overwhelmed at the idea they'd be sitting with the adults during the service instead of attending Sunday school as they did at the Mennonite church.

However, the morning service was being held in the community center attached to the church because none of the Amish had a home to invite the others to. There was

Dear Reader,

Since you are a lover of our books, your opinions are important to us... and so is your time.

That's why we made sure your **"FAST FIVE" READER SURVEY** can be completed in just a few minutes. Your answers to the five questions will help us remain at the forefront of women's fiction.

And, as a thank-you for participating, we'd like to send you up to **4 FREE BOOKS** and **FREE THANK-YOU GIFTS!**

Try **Love Inspired® Romance Larger-Print** books featuring Christian characters facing modern-day challenges.

Try **Love Inspired® Suspense Larger-Print** novels featuring Christian characters facing challenges to their faith... and lives.

Or TRY BOTH!

Enjoy your gifts with our appreciation,

Pam Powers

To get up to
4 FREE BOOKS & THANK-YOU GIFTS:

✱ Quickly complete the "Fast Five" Reader Survey
and return the insert.

"FAST FIVE" READER SURVEY

1	Do you sometimes read a book a second or third time?	○ Yes ○ No
2	Do you often choose reading over other forms of entertainment such as television?	○ Yes ○ No
3	When you were a child, did someone regularly read aloud to you?	○ Yes ○ No
4	Do you sometimes take a book with you when you travel outside the home?	○ Yes ○ No
5	In addition to books, do you regularly read newspapers and magazines?	○ Yes ○ No

YES! Please send me my Free Rewards, consisting of **2 Free Books from each series I select** and **Free Mystery Gifts**. I understand that I am under no obligation to buy anything, as explained on the back of this card.

❏ **Love Inspired® Romance Larger-Print** (122/322 IDL GNSN)
❏ **Love Inspired® Suspense Larger-Print** (107/307 IDL GNSN)
❏ **Try Both** (122/322 & 107/307 IDL GNSY)

FIRST NAME   LAST NAME

ADDRESS

APT.#   CITY

STATE/PROV.   ZIP/POSTAL CODE

no ordained minister, but she'd heard Isaac Kauffman served as his district's *vorsinger*, so he'd lead the singing.

His sister, Abby, greeted Carolyn as she and the children crossed the road in front of the community center. "Come with me," Abby said, motioning toward the women who were waiting on the right side of the building. "We women sit on one side facing the men." She smiled at the children. "You get to sit with me and your *mamm*. I mean, your mother."

Raising her chin, Rose Anne said, "I know that word. *Mamm* means mommy. *Daed* means daddy, but we don't gots one of those."

Abby gave Carolyn a stricken look. "I didn't mean to remind them of your loss."

She reassured the other woman as Rose Anne waved at Michael and his friends who stood to the left of the entrance. His clothes were the same as the ones he wore at work, but clean and pressed.

Only Isaac had on the traditional black *mutze* coat and trousers Amish men wore to church. She wondered how many bags Isaac had brought with him from the Northeast Kingdom.

"Can I sit with Michael?" Kevin pumped out his chest. "Michael is my friend. He's going to teach me to whittle."

"Is that so?" Abby smiled. "If Carolyn and Michael agree, you may sit with him, but you must stay with him throughout the whole service. You can't switch seats later."

"I want to sit with Michael." He gave Carolyn the sad puppy eyes that always matched his most heartfelt pleas. "Say it's okay. Please!"

"If it's okay with Michael…" She didn't get a chance

to add more as Kevin erupted into a run toward where the men had gathered.

She watched as Michael bent toward her nephew, listened to what Kevin had to say and then nodded. He put a gentle hand on the boy's shoulder and drew him closer to make him a part of the men's group. The happiness slipping through her battered aside the cold morning wind. Michael was what her nephew needed. A good man who treated him with kindness and offered to teach him things a boy should know. Things that, no matter how much she tried, Carolyn knew she would never comprehend in the same way.

Holding Rose Anne's hand while the women filed into the community center after the men, Carolyn wondered how a room that served as a day care center, a cafeteria and a gathering spot for volunteers discussing the next day's work could look so different when it became a place to worship. The sunlight coming through the clear glass on the tall windows made giant checkerboards across the two rows of chairs facing each other. The chairs would be more comfortable during the long service than the usual backless benches. There wasn't a bench wagon in Evergreen Corners to go from one home to the next with all the necessities for a church Sunday, including extra dishes and silverware.

She was surprised when she was handed a hymn book. Abby leaned toward her to whisper that Isaac had brought several with him.

"My big brother always worries about the smallest details," she said.

Carolyn smiled and was startled when Abby didn't. There was some undercurrent between brother and sister she couldn't understand, but she didn't ask. Not only was the service about to begin but asking too many questions about Abby's family would give tacit permission for Abby to ask about Carolyn's. That she couldn't allow.

Kevin and Rose Anne, the only children there, looked around in confusion when the congregation rose. Isaac began to sing a familiar hymn, but so slowly that Carolyn wasn't astonished the children didn't recognize the song, though they'd sung it often in Sunday school. As *vorsinger*, Isaac started each line and the rest of them joined in.

She remained silent, though she longed to sing. *Forgive me, Lord, for not raising my voice in Your praise. And forgive me for not being myself here in Your presence.*

As each verse was sung at the same deliberate tempo, Rose Anne began to fidget. Carolyn glanced across at the men and saw Kevin doing the same. Again Michael bent to whisper something to her nephew. Kevin grinned at him and stopped shuffling his feet.

Without a pause as soon as the first hymn was finished, the congregation began "*Das Loblied*," the traditional second hymn sung at each service. The words she knew so well reached into her heart and knit together some of the wounds that had opened when she left her plain life behind in Indiana. She longed more than ever to sing with the others, but resisted. To open her mouth would betray her secret. She held Rose Anne's hand while the song threaded its way through each verse.

"What are they singing about?" the little girl whispered.

"I'm sure it's about how wonderful it is to be able to worship God together," she answered as quietly.

"When will we sing 'Jesus Loves Me'?"

"We'll have to wait and see." She put her finger to the little girl's lips. "Now we need to be quiet and listen."

"To what? I can't unclestan the words."

"Maybe if you listen hard, you'll *understand* some of the words."

Abby glanced at them and smiled, never breaking the languid tempo that was so different from the four part harmony and quicker pace of Mennonite services.

Facing them from the first row of chairs on the men's side of the room, Michael had a hand around Kevin's shoulders. Her nephew gazed at him with adoration.

Uneasiness swept away her contentment and the joy that had filled her as she heard familiar hymns sung in the familiar way. She had no idea how long Michael would remain in Evergreen Corners, and her nephew was going to be devastated when he left.

You will, too.

As if on cue, both Rose Anne and Kevin became restless as soon as everyone sat so they could listen to a reading from the Bible. She drew her niece onto her lap and pulled a book out of her purse so the little girl could have something to entertain herself.

She looked across at Michael and glanced from Rose Anne's book to her brother. Michael held out his hand. She stretched across the space between the women's chairs and the men's, and gave him a book she'd packed for Kevin. Handing it to the boy, he raised his eyes toward her.

When she mouthed a silent *thank you*, she expected him to return his attention to the older Umble brother who was self-consciously reading the eighth chapter of Genesis, the verses about the flood receding and Noah emerging from the ark. Instead, his gaze held hers. Something shifted deep within her, something with the power of the story of God's grace in giving humans a second chance at redeeming themselves.

She couldn't move her gaze away. She didn't want to.

Later, though she had no idea how much time had passed as she fell into the brown warmth of his eyes, she blinked as if waking from the sweetest dream. Rose Anne was tapping on her arm to get her attention.

Carolyn knew she should be grateful to her niece for diverting her, but all she could feel was sorrow that the wonderful moment had ended. She knew, if she had an iota of good sense, she wouldn't ever let it happen again.

No matter how much her heart longed for her to.

Michael was glad the gathering was small enough that the men, women and Carolyn's *kinder* were able to sit together to share cold sandwiches and pickles and potato salad. He wasn't sure if the Wiebe *kinder* would be willing to wait if the men were served first as was customary. And he wasn't ready for them to leave.

Carolyn stood to help the others clear the table, and he edged nearer so he could talk to her without everyone else being a part of the conversation. When their gazes had collided while Vernon stumbled through the reading he'd been asked to do, Michael had been sure he'd seen more than casual interest in her eyes.

He was far less certain when she said in a tone that suggested they were strangers, "Thank you for inviting us to the service today. I hope Kevin didn't give you too much trouble. It's not easy for little ones to sit through a long service."

"He was fine." Why was she acting cool when her gaze had been filled with such warmth? He struggled to keep his own voice even. "Though he kept asking me questions about what everyone was saying and singing about."

"Rose Anne did, too, until she fell asleep."

"I hope you weren't too bored."

"I'm never bored when I'm with others who are praising God."

He was astonished as a feeling he thought he'd put aside rushed through him. The last time he'd felt anything like it was when he'd been envious of the man walking by Adah's side after she'd told him—and everyone else—she wasn't interested in Michael any longer. It'd taken months to submerge his irritation. He'd thought he'd banished it from his mind forever.

Now envy surged back as he heard Carolyn's simple statement of faith. When she turned to put a stack of plates on the pass-through to the kitchen, he saw the small round *kapp* that announced to the world—and, more important, to God—of her commitment to her faith. She knew who and what she was.

And he was no closer to having that self-assurance about what God expected of him than he'd been when he left Lancaster County to follow his twin brother to northern New York.

Knowing he couldn't let the conversation lag or she might go to talk with someone else, he said, "I suppose Abby translated for you."

"She did during the sermon Isaac gave, but the rest of the service was pretty self-explanatory." She looked past him and groaned. "Oh, Kevin! He could find mischief in an empty room."

When she whirled past him to go to where her nephew was trying to hold back boxes about to tumble out of a closet, Michael didn't follow. Two of James's brothers rushed to help her, and there wasn't room for anyone else in the cramped space.

However, after the boxes were restored in the closet and stable again, and Kevin had been chastised for peeking into places he shouldn't, Michael had the boy sit beside him on the bench at the back of the big room. The women were in the kitchen, cleaning up, and the other men were rearranging the tables so they'd be ready for breakfast tomorrow morning.

Michael pulled out his pocketknife and opened it. Kevin's eyes grew big as Michael held the haft out to him. Gripping it in his left hand, the boy watched in uncharacteristic silence as Michael picked up a broken stake. He'd cut it to about a foot in length so it'd be the right size for a *kind*.

"Are you left-handed?" he asked the boy.

Kevin looked at the knife in his left hand and shrugged.

"Which hand do you use when you're coloring or writing?"

He started to raise his left arm, but halted when Michael cautioned him.

"I wouldn't have cut you, Michael," Kevin said, chagrined.

"I know you wouldn't have intended to, but any time you're responsible for something that could hurt someone else, you must be extra, extra careful. Always think about where the blade is and where everyone and everything around you is. You'll do that, ain't so?"

Kevin nodded, as solemn as a *kind* could be. In spite of his efforts to show he was mature enough to handle the pocketknife, his face glowed with anticipation for his first whittling lesson.

"Okay, let's get started." He handed Kevin the stake

and told him how to hold it. "Always cut away from you." He guided the *kind*'s hand holding the pocketknife to a spot about halfway down the stake. "That way, if your knife slides off the wood in the wrong direction, it won't hurt you. It's a lesson you don't want to learn the hard way. Now you cut with the grain."

"Grain?"

"See the darker lines in the pine?" Michael pointed them out. "That's the direction of the grain. You should always go in that direction, because it'll be easier for both you and the wood. A slow, long stroke along the wood is best."

Kevin jammed his knife against the pine, snagging the blade. He tried to pull it back. It was stuck.

Taking the stake, Michael drew the knife out. "Make thin bites into the wood. You don't want big chunks like a piece of bread, but thin strips like a slice of cheese to put on bread. Watch me."

It wasn't easy keeping his eyes on the knife and the boy at the same time. He needed to have Kevin sit close enough that he could see, but not so near he'd get struck if the knife slid off the wood. He was sure Carolyn would put an end to the lessons if either he or Kevin nicked their fingers.

By the time the others were gathering at the far side of the room, Kevin was becoming more confident in handling the knife.

"*Gut, gut,*" Michael crooned as Kevin managed to make two shallow cuts in the wood. "You're going to be *gut* at this if you keep practicing."

Rose Anne skipped up and grinned when she saw what they were doing. "How long before Kevin can make something pretty like the little wooden bird we used to have?"

Both *kinder* looked at Michael for an answer.

"Tell me about it," he said.

"It was a hawk, which is my mommy's favorite bird."

"Is that so?"

Kevin nodded. "She says a hawk takes the gift of the wind God gives us and uses it to soar high in search of food. It will only kill what it or its babies have to have in order to eat." He cut off another piece of wood. "Unless something attacks its nest. Then it'll go after an animal bigger than it is." He shifted the knife, and a piece of wood popped off.

His sister frowned as she examined the small chunk. "You're making it flopsided."

Michael didn't hold back his laugh at the little girl's pronouncement.

Rose Anne put her hands on her hips. "It's not nice to laugh at someone."

"You're right," he replied as he smothered another chuckle at the pose that suggested she was the older one trying to instruct Michael. "But it's okay to laugh when you're with someone who makes you happy."

Her frown became a broad smile. "Do I make you happy?"

"You do."

When she spun on her heel and ran away, he wondered why. Figuring out the Wiebe women clearly was a task he couldn't master.

He looked at Kevin, who was concentrating on whittling. Before he could say a single word to the boy, Rose Anne rushed back to them. She held up a bright red box kite almost as big as she was.

"Will you help me?" she asked.

He took it. "If you want."

Rose Anne gave him another frown, but this one was easy to translate. She wouldn't have asked him if she didn't want his help.

Trying not to laugh at the expression the *kind* must have borrowed from her *mamm*, he took the knife from Kevin. He told both *kinder* to get their coats. He thought Kevin might protest, but the boy giggled with excitement when he noticed what his sister had given Michael.

He wondered where Carolyn was. He didn't see her in the kitchen. Finding Abby, he asked her to let Carolyn know he was taking the *kinder* outside to fly their kite. The youngsters bounced as they hurried outside with him.

Within a minute, they were standing in a clear section of the village green and the kite was soaring over their heads, far from the trees edging the open space. Both kids begged to hold onto the string. He could imagine a big gust sending Rose Anne skyward along with the kite. However, he gave her the first chance. He knelt beside her and kept his own hand on the string because he didn't want the little girl to get distracted and release it. On such a blustery afternoon, the kite could go sailing a distance and, once it hit the ground, be broken.

Michael took his attention from the kite when Kevin ran off. Where was the boy going? He smiled when he saw a well-bundled Carolyn walking toward them.

Why hadn't he ever noticed that the black coat she'd been given was at least two sizes too big for her? Maybe because the wind kept catching its hem and tossing it around her skirt and apron in every possible direction.

He sighed. Having her join them for the service hadn't

revealed anything new about why she seemed to be able to understand *Deitsch*. Perhaps he'd been overly optimistic in his hopes that inviting her to church would answer his questions about her once and for all because the everyday Amish language was different from the High German used during church services.

But it had revealed one vital thing: he wanted to spend more time with her.

A lot more time, more time than he'd planned to stay in Evergreen Corners. He'd told Gabriel he would be home at the first of the year, which was about six weeks away.

Carolyn smiled when she stopped next to him and Rose Anne. "When I came back in from taking out the trash, Abby told me none of you had enough good sense to stay inside where it's nice and warm."

"I was recruited to fly this kite," he said.

"I asked you to be patient, Rose Anne," Carolyn said. "You shouldn't have bothered Michael."

"She's no bother." He winked at the little girl. "And she didn't have to do any persuading. I haven't had a chance to play with a kite since I was a *kind*, so I'm glad I remembered how it works."

"It's souring, Mommy," Rose Anne announced. "See? Up there. Michael says it's souring."

When Carolyn looked baffled, Michael stood. "I think she means soaring."

"You're getting good at translating her unique form of English," she said, laughing.

A half hour later, when the sun was perched atop the western mountains, they reeled in the kite, and he watched Carolyn show Kevin how to wind the string so it could be released with ease the next time they wanted to fly it. She was such a *gut mamm*. He doubted the *kinder* had any idea how blessed they were.

He didn't ask Carolyn if he could walk home with her and the *kinder*. He strolled alongside her as Kevin and Rose Anne frolicked in front of them, their energy far from depleted. There was no traffic on the road on the late Sunday afternoon. For the first time in days, he wondered how the world beyond Evergreen Corners was faring.

Had the roads been repaired enough for traffic to get back to normal? There had been rumors on Friday about the state department of transportation coming next week to the village so every road in and out of town would once again be smooth, two-lane highways. The villagers were eager to be able to get out of town to the big box stores where the selection of food and other goods was far broader than in the small general store.

"Thank you," Carolyn said, "for making sure Kevin kept his ten fingers."

"He's a *gut* student," Michael replied as they moved from one elongated shadow to the next. "Eager to learn and cautious."

"For now. Once he's no longer in awe of the knife, he may be careless."

"Then it's my job to make sure he never loses his awe of what a blade can do." He gave a short laugh. "If I'd known he was left-handed, I might not have offered to teach him. You're right-handed. Was his *daed* left-handed?"

"No." She paused so long he wondered if he'd made a huge mistake to mention the *kind*'s *daed* before she said, "But we do have other lefties in the family. It's been a challenge teaching him some things, but we've learned to muddle through when I can't see things the way he does."

"When I watch you with your *kinder*, I find myself wondering about what it would have been like to know my own *mamm*. I don't recall much about her."

"That's sad."

He shrugged. "You can't miss what you don't remember having. I do have a few memories of my *daed*, but most of what I knew in my childhood came from living with Aden Girod. When we were eight-year-old orphans, he took Gabriel and me into his home and raised us as his own. He was a *gut* man." Michael sighed. "It was after he died that we moved from Pennsylvania to Harmony Creek Hollow."

"You miss him."

"I do." He stopped by the wooden steps leading to the old mill that now was the town hall. Someone had marked the height of the flood on the wall. It was three inches above the top of his own six feet, making it almost twenty feet above the brook's bed.

She halted and faced him. "But he's always within you."

He drew in a sharp breath when her fingertips brushed his coat over his heart. Her touch was light and so brief that, if it had been anyone else, he wouldn't have noticed. He couldn't ever be unaware of her. He didn't want to be.

"He's the one who taught me to appreciate wood," he said, needing to share this memory with her. "Once he saw I enjoyed making things by whittling, he introduced me to carpentry and woodworking. I never was interested in making furniture, but cabinets fascinated me. I liked—and still like—how a series of wooden boxes can be arranged in such a useful pattern."

"What a gift he gave you!" She began walking toward the trailer, and he matched her steps so the *kinder* didn't get too far ahead.

"I'm grateful every day he didn't hesitate to become our *daed*. He always said a family is a family, no matter how it comes into being."

"I like that." She smiled at him, and he had to clamp his arm along his side before it moved of its own accord to encircle her shoulders.

Then they were standing in front of the trailer, and he knew he needed to bid them *gut nacht* and leave before he couldn't fight his longing to pull her into his arms. He turned to the *kinder* when Carolyn prompted them to thank him. Was she as aware of the electricity arcing between them like lightning knitting together storm clouds?

Rose Anne mumbled something, but Kevin said, "Thanks for teaching me to whittle, Michael. Can we do it again tomorrow?"

"I'm not sure about tomorrow because we may be working late on your house if the weather holds, but we'll whittle again soon. *Danki* for joining us today, Kevin."

The boy stood a bit taller when Michael offered his hand. He shook it with a rare solemnity. "I hope God heard my prayers today."

"He always hears our prayers," Carolyn said in a strained voice.

Glancing from her to her son, Michael asked, "What were you praying for, Kevin?"

"That God would find Tippy and make sure he's okay. If He can't bring Tippy back to me, then I hope He finds some other boy for Tippy to spend time with. Someone who needs a best friend." Tears bubbled into his eyes as he flung the door open and ran into the trailer with Rose Anne on his heels.

Carolyn bit her lower lip, trying—and failing—to keep it from trembling.

"I'm sorry," Michael said, hating the trite words. But they were the truth. He was sorry she and the *kinder* had lost so much.

When she spoke, her voice cracked. "It's my fault that Tippy is gone. I thought I'd grabbed Kevin's stuffed dog, but in our hurry to escape, I took a blanket instead."

"By the time you realized that, it was too late to go back."

She nodded as the lights came on in the trailer, revealing her haunted eyes. "The water was already halfway to my knees in the house when I got the children out. I didn't dare go back with them, and I couldn't leave them outside alone."

"Of course you couldn't."

"Kevin's been talking more about Tippy." She closed her eyes, trying to hold in her own tears. "I know he's praying for Tippy to be returned."

"I can put the word out among the volunteers to be on the lookout for a stuffed dog."

"Thank you, but I don't want to get his hopes up only to have them dashed again."

Or your own, he thought. How much sorrow had Carolyn carried on her slender shoulders before the flood tore her life apart? How much more since?

Chapter Ten

The knock interrupted breakfast. Before Carolyn could remind Kevin she should answer the door in the trailer as she had when they'd had a house, he'd thrown it open. Not that she expected Leland at the trailer's door while it was so difficult to get into Evergreen Corners, but she couldn't let down her guard.

"Michael!" her nephew crowed as if having the man on the other side was the greatest surprise ever.

Or the best gift, because the boy began firing questions about what the construction teams would be doing and wasn't it great that Kevin didn't have school today because it was a teacher in-service day and he could join the workers and so what did Michael think he could do to help? It was all said without her nephew taking a single breath. He might have kept on going until he ran out of oxygen and keeled over right in the middle of the kitchen if she hadn't put her hands on his shoulders and turned him toward the table.

"You need to finish your breakfast," she chided, "before you think about what you're going to do today."

"I'm going to help Michael." He grinned at the man who stood on the steps into the trailer. "I am, right?"

Without looking over her shoulder, she asked before anyone else could speak, "Do you want to join us, Michael?"

"We're having flipjacks," Rose Anne announced through a full mouth of pancakes.

"Flipjacks?" asked Michael as he entered. "Another Rose Anne-ism?"

"She seems to have one for every occasion." Carolyn moved to the small stove, glad for the excuse to put some distance between herself and Michael's shoulders, which seemed wider in the cramped space. Their heartfelt discussion yesterday on the way back from the church service had created a bridge she'd been trying to keep from forming. With it now in place, she couldn't think of a way to dismantle it without hurting Michael. "Would you like pancakes, or did you eat over at the community center?"

"The line was long there, so I just grabbed a cup of *kaffi* and a couple of biscuits. If you've got enough batter, I'd appreciate some flipjacks." He gave Rose Anne a wink, and she giggled, wiggling on the bench like an adorable puppy before she moved over to give him room.

"I've made plenty, and if I run out, it's easy to mix more." She didn't look toward the table as she heard the creak of the banquette when he slid in beside the children.

Pouring batter onto the griddle, she took another plate out and listened to Michael tease her niece as Kevin kept interjecting questions about the day's work that waited at the building site.

"We'll be putting up the roof rafters today so we can begin the sheathing next week," he answered. "The house will be closed up before the weather gets much worse."

"So soon?" she asked, half turning in her excitement. The house had been a skeleton for the past few days with only her imagination filling in the spaces between the rows of two-by-fours.

"Just in time," Michael said before adding his thanks when she put the plate with two skillet-sized pancakes on the table in front of him. Reaching for the bottle of syrup, he added, "It's getting colder every day. Any rain we get now will leave everything covered with ice."

"Our autumns are beautiful in Vermont, but we sometimes have snow before the leaves are off the trees. When that happens, lots of branches come down making a mess of the roads and yards and roofs. Who would have guessed this year, instead of an early snowstorm, we'd get a late hurricane?"

"We can predict the weather a few days out, but that's about it. Even the almanacs get it wrong sometimes." He poured syrup over his pancakes, catching a drop on his finger before it could fall onto the table. Sticking his finger in his mouth, he raised his brows. "This is delicious!"

"It's maple syrup. *Real* maple syrup." She laughed. "You're in Vermont, and we don't serve anything but the real thing. It may be against the law."

Kevin sat straighter. "Really?"

"She's joking," Michael said before she could. He nudged her nephew with his elbow, and both laughed.

She was amazed how easy Kevin and Michael's relationship was. Her nephew hadn't grown close to any other man in Evergreen Corners. Should she have asked Michael right from the beginning not to let the children get too close to him? It was too late to protect them now, because they already adored him. She couldn't deny her niece and nephew the chance to enjoy his company. When the time came for her to tell them the truth about the man who was their father, she would remind them of how nice Michael had been to them, so they'd be reassured not all men were violent to those they loved.

But that was years from now, and she wished she knew a way to keep them from being heartbroken when Michael's stint of volunteering came to an end and he left.

Kevin pouted after Michael went to work without him. Climbing onto his bunk, he refused to speak to either Carolyn or his sister. Not even fresh cookies could lure him down, so she gave up trying to explain Michael couldn't be distracted while he was working.

As if Kevin's mood was infectious, Rose Anne became irritable, too. Again, Carolyn's warm cookies didn't seem to help, though her niece did try one. She acted reluctant but out of the corner of her eye Carolyn saw the little girl take two more, handing one to her brother before clambering up to join him.

Carolyn felt their eyes on her as she took the last batch of cookies out of the oven and set the cookie sheet on top of the stove. As always, she checked to make sure she hadn't accidentally turned on one of the burners. She didn't want to scorch the cookies or ruin the tray belonging to the family that was loaning them the trailer.

A yawn surprised her, but then she remembered she hadn't had a second cup of coffee that morning. She'd given the last in the pot to Michael before he went out into the cold. She decided to finish her housework. It wouldn't take long to clean the small trailer, and then she would take cookies to the volunteer builders.

Going into the bedroom, she folded their clean clothes, grateful for the washer and dryer in the trailer. Before the flood, she'd used the laundromat, toting baskets of clothes there and back each week. She'd heard it was open again. It hadn't been flooded, but the water supply had been cut off for a couple of weeks. She put the clothing in the appropriate drawers. As always, the children's looked as if they'd pawed to the bottom every day. She glanced into the single drawer she used, and it wasn't much neater. They didn't have a lot of clothing, but they could have used more storage.

Carolyn walked back into the main room of the trailer. "Let's go…"

The children were nowhere to be seen.

"Kevin? Rose Anne?" she called.

She didn't get any answer. Opening the closet, she saw their coats, mittens and hats were gone.

Carolyn knew where the children would be. Kevin was fascinated with the building process and wouldn't stay away from Michael. Rose Anne was interested because her big brother was. The little girl had been trailing after her brother from the time she could walk. Both of them knew the rules for crossing the street, and before the flood Kevin had begun to walk the short distance to the elementary school on his own.

Grabbing her own coat, she pulled it on and hurried down the hill. She shivered in the icy wind as she watched a large delivery truck drive past where she stood on the sidewalk near the library. She tried to keep her skirt from flying up as the truck rushed by her. Dust rose from the road covered with dried mud. It seemed every rain storm brought more loose soil onto the narrow line of asphalt. Until the ground froze, it would repeat with each storm. She grimaced as she thought of how it would begin again with the first spring thaw.

But by then, she and Kevin and Rose Anne would

have moved into their new home. She'd heard during breakfast that the diner was under repair and the owners hoped to have it open by the New Year. If so, she hoped they would again buy baked goods from her, so she could save for the furniture and clothes her family would need in the coming months.

By then, too, Michael and the other volunteers would be long gone.

Every joyous thought she had of living in a real house again was tinged with sadness at knowing he would have returned to his own home. Her memories of the meals he'd shared with her and the children in the trailer gathered around her with each breath. Brushing them away was impossible, because she wanted to hold them close. They banished the pain of seeing *Mamm* belittled and Regina abused and her own life shadowed by threats of the same violence.

She waved aside the dust, coughing and scowling as she saw the fine layer clinging to her black coat. Shaking it off, she crossed the road once the truck had disappeared around a corner. She followed the brownish cloud past where Rhee's cellar was now topped off by sheets of plywood ready for the framing to begin.

Nobody was on that site, so she kept going. The Gagnons' site was also abandoned, but she heard noise from hers. Rushing forward, she glanced around, searching for her nephew and niece. When she saw them standing with Benjamin by the pen where the hens now lived, she breathed a grateful prayer. She didn't look forward to scolding the children, but they must learn they couldn't run off.

As she walked toward them, she couldn't resist a look at the house. On the far side, men were hauling large sections of rafters up to form the roof. It was exciting to see the house take shape.

She bowed her head to send up more heartfelt gratitude to God Who had sent these helping hands to Evergreen Corners. She wasn't sure what she would have done otherwise.

Raising her eyes, she saw Michael standing on the far side of the house. His gaze connected with hers, and she forgot about rafters and concrete and breathing. Her pulse resonated in her ears. She wasn't sure if he moved first or if she did, but somehow by taking a few steps, she found they were standing face-to-face.

"Hi," she said.

"Hi," he answered.

She gazed at the slow smile that eased the tense lines of his wind-scoured face. A delightful warmth flickered within her, and she leaned toward him, halting when the mittens she hadn't realized she was holding instead of wearing struck his hard chest.

Somehow, she collected the tattered remnants of her composure and said, "I'm here to find two naughty children."

He smiled. "I thought that might be why you're here with your coat unbuttoned and without your bonnet." He laughed when she touched the round *kapp* on her hair. "When I saw them arrive, I assumed you wouldn't be far behind."

"They slipped out when I wasn't looking."

"I was worried they might do something like that. I've been sprinting back and forth from here to the road between helping lift each rafter. I was about to believe they had better sense than to take off without you when I saw them. Benjamin and I have been taking turns watching over them."

"Thank you."

"It was my pleasure."

Michael realized the trite words were true. He'd been happy to keep an eye out for Kevin and Rose Anne... and Carolyn.

"James and his brothers left this morning to return home," he said to keep the conversation going. "He needed to go back to Harmony Creek Hollow and his work as a blacksmith because our *Leit* depends on him to shoe their horses."

"Maybe his brothers didn't want to stay when he wasn't here for them to boss around."

"Why, Carolyn Wiebe, what a thing for a *gut* Mennonite to say!"

"We're taught to speak the truth." When he grinned, she hurried to add, "And the truth is I'm grateful for everyone's help."

"James said to tell you he'll be back after the New Year. By then, Glen will have us starting on a new trio of houses. James's skill with metal will be valuable for the steel-reinforced concrete in the cellar walls."

She looked at the work site that was humming with activity. "So you're short-handed now?"

"No, a group of plain folks arrived this morning from Pennsylvania and were waiting here for us when we got to work. We have about a half dozen extra sets of hands here, and the two women have gone to help at the community center."

"Good. I'll meet them when—"

Shouts came from every direction. The voices were

swallowed by a great crash and the clatter of wood against stone and concrete.

Carolyn's eyes were riveted on a stack of boards falling in what seemed like slow motion. Her niece stood too close to it. She saw Benjamin leap forward to grab the little girl. Both of them vanished in a cloud of dirt and dust.

For a moment, it was so silent the brook's gurgling was the loudest sound. Then the air exploded with shouts and pounding feet as everyone ran toward the spot where Benjamin and Rose Anne had been visible seconds ago.

With her feet moving before she had a chance to think, Carolyn pushed through the others to reach her niece. She gave a sharp cry of dismay when she saw the little girl lying on the ground while Benjamin was pushing himself up to sit. Their faces were gray with pain.

"Rose Anne!" She knelt by her niece who was staring at the collapsed stack of wood as if she couldn't believe it had moved. "Are you all right?"

Instead of answering, Rose Anne shifted her gaze from the wood to her left arm. It hung at a grotesque angle, as if she had a second elbow between her wrist and her real elbow.

"Don't move," Carolyn cautioned.

"Mommy!"

"Hush, sweetheart. Just be still." Looking up, she saw Michael behind her. Kevin stood next to him, his face as pale as his sister's. She met her nephew's eyes steadily. "Her arm is broken."

Michael's head swiveled as he glanced at his friend.

Benjamin said in a strained voice, "You need to get her to a *doktor* and get it set before she does more damage to it."

"There isn't a doctor in Evergreen Corners," she said.

"Where...?" asked Michael.

"The closest one is at the urgent care clinic. It's on Route 100 heading north toward Ludlow."

"So let's go."

She stared at him. "We can't. The bridge is still out between here and there."

He'd started to turn, but halted. "There's got to be something we can do."

More shouts and a loud sob from Rose Anne kept her from answering. Looking through the open walls of their home, she saw a dark-haired woman hurrying toward them. She wore the pleated *kapp* of a horse-and-buggy Mennonite. Her steps were uneven, because she wore a plastic brace on her right leg over her black stockings.

"Over here!" Carolyn called when she realized the woman was carrying a medical bag.

The crowd edged back to let the dark-haired woman past. She looked from Rose Anne to Benjamin, then knelt beside Carolyn and her niece.

"I'm Beth Ann Overholt," the woman said as she ran her hands along Rose Anne's sides and tilted her head with gentle hands. "Look at me, little one." She pulled a light from her bag and flashed it in the child's eyes. "Good. It doesn't look as if she was hit on the head."

"Are you a doctor?" Carolyn asked.

The woman shook her head as she stood and went to give Benjamin the same examination. "No. I'm a midwife."

"Midwife?" Benjamin's face twisted, and he clamped his mouth shut when her fingers brushed against his right side. Any color his face had vanished.

Beth Ann sat on her heels. "I've had enough medical training to know the two of you need to see a doctor immediately. Your ribs are, at best, bruised. At worst, you've broken one or more."

"I thought I'd jumped back far enough," he said, breathing shallowly as if he'd run the full length of the Green Mountains. "I miscalculated."

Surprised anyone could make a joke while injured, Carolyn fought to keep frustration and fear from her voice. "How do we get them to a doctor? An ambulance will take too long to get here."

Michael asked, "Didn't Glen tell us he's got a vehicle that can navigate the rough path through the woods between here and Route 100?"

"How rough?" She glanced down at the little girl whose face was growing taut with pain.

"Rough," he replied, "but it's the only way to get her to a *doktor* now."

"Where's Glen? Have you seen him today?"

He hooked a thumb toward the village. "Probably in his office."

"I'll get him!" shouted a man from the back of the crowd. She didn't see who it was before he ran to get the project director.

With every bit of care she could muster, Carolyn lifted Rose Anne into her arms. She cradled her as she had when her niece was a newborn, but made sure she didn't bump her broken arm. Kevin looked on, horrified, as Michael and Isaac assisted Benjamin to his feet.

Again the volunteers stepped aside as Carolyn carried her niece toward the road. Quiet words of good wishes and offers of prayers flanked her, and she nodded her thanks while she kept her eyes on where she placed her feet. She didn't want to slip and jar the little girl, adding to her pain. She wished she had another arm to put around Kevin as she heard him crying.

She spared a look over her shoulder and was relieved to see Michael had one arm supporting his friend and the other on Kevin's shoulder as they followed her to the road. She knew her nephew had no idea how precious Michael's consoling touch was, and that lifted her heart, which had plummeted into her stomach when she saw Rose Anne disappear as the stack of wood gave way. Kevin trusted Michael and she wanted to, as well.

More than she'd imagined she'd ever be willing to trust a man. She waited for the warning that should have flashed through her at that thought. When it didn't come, she told herself it was because she had more important things to worry about.

Like making sure Rose Anne's arm was set before it could be more badly injured. It was easier to concentrate on that than her feelings, which she'd been sure would never alter…even so slightly.

Michael made sure Benjamin was steady when they reached the road. Only then did he bend and draw out a handkerchief and give it to Kevin, who was sniffling as thick tears ran down his cheeks.

"Everything's going to be okay," Michael said as he squatted in front of the boy.

"She's broken."

"*Ja*, but God was wise when He made us. We can be fixed as *gut* as new."

"What if Tippy is broken, too? Who's taking care of him?" Kevin's eyes grew round. "God is, isn't He?"

"*Ja*." He gave the boy a quick hug. To keep Kevin from asking more questions—especially ones he couldn't answer—Michael added, "For now, though, let's get your sister and Benjamin fixed. Okay?"

"Okay."

As he stood, he saw Carolyn watching him.

She whispered, "Thank you."

He nodded, not wanting to say more in front of the *kinder*. He thought about offering to take Rose Anne, but knew Carolyn would be worried about bumping the little girl's arm during the transfer. Then he knew what he wanted to do was put his arms around Carolyn and comfort her.

When Glen rushed along the road toward them, Michael released a quick breath of relief. Fighting his own desire to hold Carolyn was becoming more difficult with each passing minute.

Glen frowned at the sight of Rose Anne in Carolyn's arms. "How bad is it?"

"A broken arm," Michael answered. "And Benjamin has done some damage to his ribs. We need to get them to a *doktor*. Carolyn tells me the closest one is out on Route 100."

"Take my 4x4 truck. It's the only vehicle that can make it through the woods. Can you drive, Michael?"

"I did a bit in the fields when I was a teenager."

"That's not the same as driving a utility vehicle on a busy road." The project director turned to Carolyn. "You know how to drive, don't you?"

"Yes."

Fishing in his pocket, he pulled out a single key on a simple chain and handed it to her. "Then you drive. We can't chance wrecking our sole emergency vehicle. Sorry, Michael."

"I'm glad to have Carolyn drive as long as she'll trust me with Rose Anne."

He wasn't surprised to see a myriad of emotions swirl through her eyes. As protective as she was of the *kind*, she was battling with herself over letting him hold her daughter during the trip to the *doktor*'s office.

Sorrow hammered him. She must have been hurt by someone she'd thought she could rely on! Her husband? The thought unsettled him further. He hadn't asked any questions about Carolyn's husband, and he wondered, as he hadn't before, if she never spoke of the *kinder*'s *daed* because he had been a disappointment to her during their lives together. Was the secret she hid that her husband had done something to betray her faith in his love for her and the *kinder*?

Michael was glad the next few minutes became a whirlwind of activity that kept him from being able to ponder those tough questions further. The 4x4, a garish green truck with two sets of bright yellow seats and a flat board over the back wheels to allow for cargo to be strapped on it, was brought to the building site. Kevin was sent with Beth Ann, who agreed to take him to the day care center. Jenna would watch him until they returned to Evergreen Corners. Workers began gathering the wood, sorting the ruined pieces and restacking the unbroken ones.

With utmost care, Carolyn slid Rose Anne into Michael's arms. The little girl began to screech with pain and thrash, but her *mamm* remained calm, stroking her daughter's hair back from her face and murmuring to her until Rose Anne stopped tossing herself against him.

What an amazing woman Carolyn Wiebe was! In the midst of any catastrophe, she was serene.

He walked behind her toward the truck, then looked back. "Aren't you coming with us, Benjamin?"

"There's nothing a *doktor* can do for bruised ribs." He winced on every word.

"They may be broken."

"Nothing a *doktor* can do for that, either. When my older brother cracked a rib, he was told to take it easy and…" He groaned.

Carolyn scowled as she slipped behind the wheel of the truck. "Enough! Get in, Benjamin!" She inserted the key into the ignition, and pulled the seat belt around her and snapped it into place.

"You heard the lady," Michael said, motioning with his head toward the vehicle. "Do you need help getting in, Benjamin?"

"I'll manage."

Michael suspected his friend regretted his hasty words as Benjamin's face grew more ashen while he pulled himself into the back seat. Pretending not to notice because he didn't want to embarrass the other man, Michael slid onto the other front seat without jostling Rose Anne.

"Put your feet on the seat, Benjamin," Carolyn urged impatiently.

"My boots—"

"Don't worry about something that can be cleaned later." Her voice softened as she added, "Putting up your feet will relieve the tension on your ribs and maybe ease your ride a little bit."

"Danki," Benjamin murmured as he shifted with care.

"All set?" she asked.

Michael knew he wasn't the only one not being honest when he replied, *"Ja."*

He looked down at the *kind* curled against him. The trip was going to be rough on each one of them, but this little one most of all.

Chapter Eleven

Michael guessed someone had called ahead to let the medical clinic know they were on their way. There had been plenty of time, because it'd been slow going through the woods on a path strewn with rocks and branches. On each bump—and there had been so many he'd lost count—he'd seen Carolyn wince.

The ride was smoother when they turned onto the highway, but the adults were kept busy watching for cars behind them. When possible, she drew the truck over onto the shoulder to let cars pass them. Several cars beeped at her when there wasn't a place to edge to the right, and he realized they weren't *gut*-natured honks.

He wanted to shout to the occupants of what Carolyn called a glorified golf cart on steroids that they were in a hurry, too. He didn't, not wanting to upset her or their injured passengers.

As soon as she steered the vehicle into the parking lot of a pristine single-story building, the front door was thrown open. Two people wearing long white coats emerged, a man and a woman. He wasn't sure which one was the *doktor*. Maybe both were because they went to work examining Rose Anne and Benjamin.

Questions were fired at him and Carolyn. He had to let her answer everything about her daughter, and Benjamin, though in more pain with each passing second, was able to share information about medical allergies and what had happened as well as Michael could. As soon as the man and woman realized that, they ignored him.

The woman lifted Rose Anne off his lap and carried her into the clinic with Carolyn following close behind.

"Can you help?" asked the white-coated man.

Michael realized he'd been staring after Carolyn and not paying attention to the conversation in the rear of the vehicle. "Me?"

"It'll be easier if one of us is on each side of Benjamin while he goes inside." The *doktor* looked at him as if he wondered if Michael had been injured, too. A head injury would make him incapable of being able to discern the most obvious thing.

"Certainly." He swung out of the vehicle and followed the *doktor*'s instructions to stand beside them as Benjamin slid out.

Michael heard his friend grunt in pain on each step as they walked to the clinic. He continued to pray. He'd reassured Kevin their injuries were easily repairable, and he didn't want to disappoint the boy.

Inside, the clinic looked like any he'd visited. On the sterile white walls hung pictures of scenery that could have been Vermont or anywhere else with mountains. A glass enclosure cut the space in half. He counted four desks on the far side, but only two were occupied.

The chairs in the waiting room were empty, and he sat in the closest one to the door through which the *doktor* led Benjamin. As he'd guessed, the chairs had been selected for their clean lines. Straight backs and seats too low to the floor made him sit at an uncomfortable angle. Unadorned side tables held magazines and a few games for *kinder*. A pair of televisions hung high on the wall and broadcast health information without sound. He ignored them and stared at the door Benjamin had used.

Time moved at a snail's pace as he sat by himself. He'd hoped someone would come out and give him an update, but the doors remained closed. Maybe he shouldn't have insisted on Kevin remaining in Evergreen Corners. He would have enjoyed the boy asking him the hundred and one questions Kevin seemed to have each day. At least that would have made the time move. He looked at the clock and was ready to assert it was running backward.

The door to the parking lot opened, and two men came in. One was supporting the bloody hand of the other. They went to the desk. The woman there took one look at the man's hand and told them to follow her. A soft buzz unlocked the door, and they vanished through it.

He waited for the door to open again with news about Rose Anne and Benjamin. It didn't happen. A man he hadn't seen before walked out, stopped at the desk and did some paperwork before he left holding several pages. He wondered how many people were being treated.

Bring each of them Your healing, God, he prayed, halting when the outer door opened again.

Three more patients entered, each one with a companion. Two, one man and one elderly woman, were suffering from bad colds, and he couldn't guess what had brought the third one, a man with a bushy brown beard, to the clinic. In turn, each of them was called to the back.

And still nobody came out.

"Are you the father of the little girl?" called the woman behind the window.

He faced her. "No, a friend." He gave her a wry grin. "To both of your patients from Evergreen Corners."

"All right. I'll take the paperwork to her mother." She rose and left before he could ask if there was any update.

Not that she would have told him anyhow. Such information was overseen by so many privacy laws that he'd need signed permission from Carolyn in order to hear the answers. That he'd held the little girl all the way to the clinic didn't matter.

But what if he were to become Rose Anne's *daed*?

He shook that out of his head. Nothing had changed. He couldn't make a commitment to anyone until he decided what his commitment to God would be.

Have you put off making up your mind on one issue so you can avoid making up your mind on the other?

He sat straighter as the unexpected thought resonated through him. He needed to be baptized before he wed. Had he been using God as an excuse to keep his heart barricaded away from another woman who would toss it aside and stomp on it publicly as Adah had? In an effort to avoid more drama, was he shutting himself away from the parts of life he should be relishing now?

The door opened, saving him from having to answer his own silent questions. Benjamin inched into the waiting room. He moved more tentatively than before.

Michael jumped to his feet and assisted his friend to an armless chair. He didn't want to chance Benjamin bumping himself as he sat.

"How bad is it?" asked Michael.

"Two broken ribs and another that's cracked." Benjamin gave a wry grin as he lowered himself into the chair. "I don't do anything halfway, I guess."

"Sorry."

His friend started to wave away the sympathy, but his breath caught as he moved his right arm. "I guess I'm going to be left-handed for a while."

"Did you see Carolyn and Rose Anne back there?"

"No. All the doors were closed. I didn't see anyone other than the *doktors* who examined me and their nurses."

Though he was anxious to hear about Rose Anne, Michael asked, "What did the *doktor* say?"

"He gave me some pain pills and told me to take them. When I said I don't like taking medicine, he said it's important because I need to be able to breathe normally. Shallow breathing can bring on pneumonia."

"You need to listen to the *doktor*."

"Easy for you to say. You're not the one who's going to be sitting around while everyone else is working." He closed his eyes. "The *doktor* said I can get back to light duty in about two weeks. He's got instructions for me to take home."

As if on cue, the receptionist called, "Mr. Kuhns?"

"I'll get it," Michael said, jumping up again.

The woman handed him a clipboard with several pages on it and a pen. She told him he could have Benjamin tell him the answers and sign it for his friend.

Fifteen minutes later, Michael knew more about Benjamin than he'd ever thought he would. He'd written down information about when his friend had snagged his finger on a fish hook and had to have stitches, as well as a broken finger when he was a teenager. Taking off the advisory pages the doctor had sent out for Benjamin to use during his recovery, Michael signed the papers and gave them back to the nurse.

"Do you know how much longer Mrs. Wiebe and her daughter will be?" he asked.

"I'm sorry, sir. I don't have that information." She took the clipboard and turned to her computer.

Michael forced himself to sit, though he longed to work off his nervous energy by pacing. He didn't want to disturb the others waiting in the silent room. Beside him, Benjamin sat, panting as if he'd run a marathon.

The door opened again, and the man with the bloody hand came out. He and his companion left. They were followed by the woman who'd been coughing hard when she arrived and a man who was probably her husband.

At last, the door swung open and a wheelchair came out. Rose Anne sat in it, her smile shaky. She was excited to be able to ride in the chair, but was hurting too much to enjoy it. The cover over the cast running from her left wrist to her elbow was the brightest pink he'd ever seen.

Carolyn stepped aside as the door opened again, and the bearded man emerged. He glanced at the wheelchair, scowled and edged around it as if it had been put intentionally in his way. He stared at Michael and Benjamin, and Michael guessed the *Englischer* had never seen a plain man before.

Michael ignored the stranger, who hurried to the receptionist's desk. Kneeling beside the wheelchair, he asked, "How's the bravest girl in Evergreen Corners?"

"Bravest?" Rose Anne's eyes glistened as her smile grew a bit stronger. "Me?"

"*Ja*, you've been as brave as your *mamm*, who is the bravest woman I know."

He watched that adorable color rise in Carolyn's too-pale face before she said, "I need to get Rose Anne's paperwork. I'll be right back."

"We'll be right here." He continued to talk to the little girl who seemed to be fading off to sleep. Putting his hand under her head, he kept it from drooping forward and leaving her with a pain in her neck as well as her arm.

After what seemed a ridiculously long time, the bearded man finished his business at the window and left, looking back to stare once more. Michael again paid him no mind.

A few minutes later, Carolyn returned and gazed down at her daughter.

"The doctor gave her something for the pain while he set the bone and cast it," she said.

"And let her pick out the cast cover?"

"Once she saw the pink, she didn't want to look at anything else. I was tempted to suggest the bright green because that would have made her visible when she's near the work site."

"I don't think anyone's going to miss seeing that pink."

"The doctor assured me it'll darken as the cast gets dirty." She sighed. "I'm going to have to figure out how to keep *her* clean for the next six weeks. You know she won't miss coming to the new house any chance she can. She's as excited as Kevin about the construction, and she misses helping me collect the chickens' eggs."

"Another reason to pray rain stays away for the next few weeks."

She smiled, and his heart began to beat at a crazy speed, as it had when he saw the wood falling. But this sensation was pleasurable.

He reached across the chair and took her hand between

his. Her fingers stiffened, then uncurled like a waking butterfly. He cupped them as if they were as fragile.

"Let's get the little one," he said, not wanting to rouse Rose Anne by saying her name, "and Benjamin home."

"Yes, let's go home," she whispered, and he found himself imagining other questions he could pose that she would say yes to.

The day's light was fading into twilight when Carolyn trudged up the hill to the trailer along with Benjamin and Michael, who was carrying Rose Anne. Jenna was waiting with Kevin and her daughter, Taylor. The librarian insisted on taking Benjamin to her neighbor's house.

"I checked with them," Jenna said. "It was the least I could do after all the help you've given to me at the library in the past week. My neighbors, the Zielinskis, have an extra bed in their den for you. You remember them, right? They emptied their big chest freezer so we could put books in there to keep them from getting moldy. The Zielinskis agree you shouldn't sleep in a barn while dealing with your injury."

"I'll be fine there." His voice remained wispy, and Carolyn noticed how hard he seemed to be struggling for each breath.

Michael must have heard that, too, because he said in his most no-nonsense voice, "Don't try to be a hero, Benjamin. These people want to help you. Let them."

"Listen to Michael," Carolyn said, not wanting the debate to keep her from her children. "Basia and Walter are wonderful people, and they've been disappointed they haven't been able to help. They're elderly, so can't do much as far as the rebuilding or cleanup. However, they'll keep you on your toes, Benjamin. Don't let them talk you into playing trivia. You're guaranteed to lose."

Benjamin nodded reluctantly. "All right. It's not easy to accept charity from someone I've never met."

"Isn't that what I did when you and Michael and the others came to Evergreen Corners to rebuild my house? We'd never met."

"Seems hard to believe, ain't so?" Michael said as he carried a drowsy Rose Anne into the trailer and set her on the sofa bed that Jenna had open and ready for her. "Benjamin, you're skilled with making things from the wood pieces left over at your sawmill. You can make them something nice to repay them." His brows lowered again. "Once you're feeling better again."

Carolyn took the plate of cookies she'd intended to deliver to the building site that morning. Such a short time ago. It seemed as if it'd been a week since she'd gone flying out of the trailer after the children. Now Kevin sat too quietly in the bunk, and Rose Anne was lying on her bed, her little face wrinkled with pain. And Carolyn's own nerves were taut, making every word and every action vibrate along them.

"Here. Take these with you." She held out the plate to Jenna. "Basia always asks when I'm going to make oatmeal date cookies again."

"Oatmeal date?" asked Michael, and she noticed his voice sounded as casual as she'd tried to make hers. Was he hiding behind a facade as she was? Whether he was or not, she appreciated his sanding the edges off the tension in the trailer. "I've never heard of them."

"I got the recipe from Abby."

"Isaac's sister?" Jenna asked.

Carolyn nodded, glad her friend didn't ask any more

questions before she took the plate and motioned for Benjamin to follow her and Taylor, who'd been silent as she stared at the cast on Rose Anne's arm.

Carolyn closed the door in their wake. Though she wished she could lose herself in sleep as her niece had, she must offer Kevin solace. Her nephew had been as quiet as Taylor, and that wasn't like him. She climbed into his bunk and, despite the cramped space, huddled with him. Putting her arms around him, she listened as he wept out his terror that she and Rose Anne wouldn't come back. She consoled him in the gentle whispers that always reached through his fear, knowing the day's events had dredged up the one when she'd had to tell him his *mamm* couldn't be with him again until he joined her in heaven. Though she'd done all she could to take Regina's place, her nephew's scars hadn't healed.

When he admitted he was hungry, a sure sign he was feeling better, Carolyn climbed out of the bunk. Michael lifted Kevin down to sit at the table so he didn't disturb his little sister, and told him about the drive through the woods until the worst of the fright had vanished from her nephew's face. At the same time, Carolyn heated the leftover soup she'd planned for their midday meal. She realized Kevin was the only one who'd had anything to eat since breakfast. She let Rose Anne sleep while she served the soup and grilled cheese sandwiches, but she left the teakettle simmering.

Through the meal, Michael kept the conversation light until Kevin yawned. Sending the boy to get ready for bed and reminding him to brush his teeth and wash his face—"With soap this time, Kevin!"—she cleared the table. She was shocked she'd finished every bite in her bowl and on her plate.

When Kevin closed the bathroom door, Michael stood and took a cup from the cupboard. He poured hot water over a tea bag from the box on the shelf over the sink. "Do you need help getting Rose Anne ready for bed?"

"I think I'll let her sleep. It'd be a shame to wake her up to put on her pajamas. I saved some soup in case she wakes later and is hungry."

"Do you think she'll sleep through the night?"

"I hope so." Her gaze met his. "I need to tell you again how grateful I am, Michael, that you and Benjamin and James let us use this trailer. I don't know how we would have managed in the stables."

"You would have found a way." He handed her the steaming cup of tea. "I suspect you always do."

She lowered her eyes. What would he say if she revealed the truth of the past four years?

If he noticed her action, he didn't speak of it as Kevin came out of the bathroom. Michael waited for her to listen to her nephew's nightly prayers, which now included a request every night for Tippy to come back, and then lifted the boy into his bunk.

Once she knew Kevin was asleep, Carolyn went to hang up their coats, which had been tossed on her bed. When she heard the crackle of papers in her pocket, she took out the sheets the receptionist had given her. She sorted them, putting the ones for Rose Anne's care to one side so she could refer to them during the next six weeks until her cast could be removed.

She flipped over one of the pages and gasped.

"Was iss letz?" asked Michael.

So shaken she didn't care he'd spoken in *Deitsch*, she replied, "I didn't realize until I looked at the forms they gave me at the clinic. Today is exactly one month from the night of the flood."

He stepped forward and drew her into his arms. She leaned her cheek over his heart. Its pace jumped as her own had when he touched her. Being held to him was like coming home after wandering, lost, for all her life. She closed her eyes and drank in the scent of him.

"I'm sorry," he murmured against her hair. "If I'd realized, I would have... I don't know what I would have done, but I wish I could make this easier for you."

"You are." Her arms curved up his back as she nestled closer. She might be acting like the greatest fool in history, but she didn't care. The comfort he offered was what she hadn't realized she'd been looking for. "You're making it easier by being here."

"I'm glad." His voice was low and husky, inviting her to stay where she was as long as she wanted.

But she drew back, knowing if she remained enfolded to him she wouldn't ever want to leave. All too soon he would be returning to his own home, and their lives might never intersect again. Before he'd come to Evergreen Corners, she would have told herself it was for the best...and she would have believed it.

Now she wasn't sure what to believe.

Chapter Twelve

Michael pulled his scarf around his collar and listened to the muffled clank of his tool belt beneath his heavy coat. He'd heard the winters in Vermont were rougher than what he was used to in Pennsylvania, but hearing it and living it were two different things. In the week since the accident on the work site, it seemed every morning was much, much colder than the previous day.

Benjamin was spending time at the library helping Jenna and other volunteers determine what was salvageable and what had been ruined beyond repair. He'd returned to the stables after two nights at the Zielinskis' house, grateful for their hospitality but overwhelmed by Basia's determination to coddle him as if he were her own *kins-kind*.

Each day, Michael got updates on Rose Anne from Kevin, who seemed to appear wherever he was working. The little girl was already complaining about wearing a heavy cast, because it kept her from chasing after her brother.

The previous evening, when he'd given Kevin another lesson in whittling after supper at the trailer, the boy hadn't been able to talk about anything but when it would start snowing. He couldn't wait to go sledding. The fact he no longer had a sled didn't bother him because he was planning to go with his best friend.

"My best *kid* friend," he'd told Michael. "You're my best *grown-up* friend."

Michael had heard Carolyn laugh at the comment, and he'd acknowledged what he'd been trying to ignore. He liked being in Evergreen Corners and spending time with the Wiebe family.

He liked it a lot.

A real lot.

"What if I don't want to go back to Harmony Creek Hollow?" he mused aloud, the wind snatching the words away as soon as he spoke them.

He kicked a stone along the asphalt and listened as it tumbled over the broken side of the road. Why should he leave when he'd discovered someone who—other than not being Amish—fit the criteria he would have looked for in a wife? Carolyn was kind and funny and, most important, calm.

When he'd first stepped off the bus, he'd assumed her serenity was because she was numb from the shock of the flood. His opinion had changed in the wake of her daughter's broken arm. Carolyn had been as imperturbable as one of the trees growing along the road through the whole disaster and in the days afterward. A bit subdued, perhaps, but cheerful and optimistic…and calm.

Had God brought him here in answer to his questions about his future? He was beginning to think so.

"Hey, Michael!"

At Kevin's familiar shout, Michael looked back to see Carolyn and the *kinder* walking toward him. Rose Anne seemed to be moving more naturally each day as she adjusted to her cast, which was hidden beneath a bulky coat so big the hem dropped below her knees.

"Aren't you supposed to be in school now?" he asked the boy, though his gaze settled on Carolyn, who looked lovelier than usual with her cheeks rosy from the cold.

"Tomorrow's Thanksgiving!" Kevin crowed. "We had only a half day."

"So you decided to take a walk?"

"We decided to remind ourselves," Carolyn answered before her son could, "what we're grateful for."

"The freezing weather?"

"Not that." She gestured along the road. "We're grateful for everyone who has come to work so hard on our new house."

"Have you seen it since the shingles were put on?"

Her eyes twinkled with excitement. "No! Can we go now?"

The work site was empty because the crews were doing framing and setting the rafters in place on the Gagnons' house next door. Michael smiled as the family delighted in the sight of what looked like a house now. Spaces for windows and doors had been cut into the sheathing, and he pointed out where each room would be. His face ached with his grin, because he wasn't sure who was more excited: the *kinder* or Carolyn…or himself.

Rose Anne flung her uninjured arm around his leg and hugged it. "I love my new house." She looked at him. "Can we make it a pretty color?"

"Whatever color your *mamm* wants it to be."

"How about sky-blue pink?" the little girl asked.

"We'll see what we can find at the paint store." He winked at Carolyn over Rose Anne's head.

Carolyn took her daughter's hand. "We've got to go one step at a time. Remember? We've talked about this. Wood first and then paint."

"I know. I know." The *kind*'s voice took on a world-weary tone. "We gots to follow plopper pole-scissors."

"Yes, *proper procedures* are important."

Michael put a hand over his mouth before he could burst out laughing. He was glad Carolyn had "translated" that Rose Anne-ism.

When he strode down the hill to the stack of wood he'd helped Carolyn pull out of the water when he first came to Evergreen Corners, Kevin bounced after him.

"What are you doing? Can I help?" the boy asked.

"Ja." He looked across the grassless yard to where Carolyn was guiding Rose Anne closer to the chicken pen. "We'll let them keep the chickens distracted while you and I build your chickens a new home."

"Now?" Kevin let off a cheer that set the chickens to racing around, frightened, in their pen.

"Remember what I've told you about being quiet and careful around tools?"

The *kind* froze, then nodded. "I'll be quiet."

"And careful."

"Yep."

Picking up two long planks, Michael lifted them to his shoulder as he walked toward the house. "Where would you like your henhouse, Carolyn?"

"Near the fallen log would be good. The ground is flat, and it's far enough from the house so the smell won't invade when we open the windows. Yet it'll be close enough for collecting eggs. But you don't have to do this today."

"Why not?" he asked as he put the boards on the

ground. "If Kevin can have a half day off from school, I should be able to take a half day off from work."

"So you can do different work?"

He liked how her eyes shone when she teased him. "You know what Proverbs says about idle hands, ain't so?"

"All right, but I can't stay to help. I was supposed to be at the kitchen to work on preparations for tomorrow's big feast about fifteen minutes ago."

Though he wished she wouldn't go, he nodded. "Don't let me make you later."

"We're having a gathering tonight at the community center to count our blessings as well as peel and cook all the potatoes we need. Why don't you come and join us?"

"So I can help peel potatoes?"

"I'm sure you'll be exempt after your work out here today."

He nodded. "I'll see you then."

"Can I stay and help?" Kevin asked as Carolyn motioned for her son to come with her.

"It's fine with me, Carolyn. Anytime." Michael was surprised how much he hoped those words would prove to be true. If he remained in Evergreen Corners...

He silenced that thought as he watched Carolyn walk toward the road with her daughter. He'd promised to build the chicken coop, so he'd better get to it before the sun set, making the air colder.

Until Kevin asked him what the song was, Michael didn't realize he was whistling as he collected a few discarded two-by-fours and began to measure them. He couldn't remember the last time he'd whistled. Back when he was a carefree kid? Then he realized it'd been before

Adah had dumped him. He'd let her melodrama steal his happiness and leave him in a grim place.

Now he wanted to whistle like a robin welcoming back spring.

He worked with the boy to complete the structure for the small building. Located where it was, it wouldn't be in the way of finishing Carolyn's house, and the chickens would be protected from the cold tonight. He built a roof, but just set it on top without attaching it to the coop. After Thanksgiving, he'd find some time to remove the roof and put in a shelf where nest boxes could be set.

"Hey, Michael," Kevin said as he sat on the log. "You know what?"

"What?" He squatted to cut out a doorway. A small piece of plank on simple hinges would allow access to the interior but allow Carolyn to shut in the chickens if she needed to.

"I hate my name."

"Why?" He looked back at the boy. "It's a *gut* name. When I lived in Pennsylvania and was about your age, I had a friend named Kevin."

"That's the problem," the boy grumbled.

"That I had a friend named Kevin?" Sometimes the course of the *kind*'s thoughts eluded him as much as the meaning of Rose Anne's odd words.

"No! The problem is I don't want to share my name." Kevin jumped to his feet, his small fists pressed closed by his sides. "Not with that stupid, stupid hurricane."

He kept measuring the doorway. "Why? The storm has come and gone, and there won't ever be another one named Kevin."

"But everyone talks about Hurricane Kevin. Sometimes they just say Kevin, and I think they're talking to me. Then I realize they're not. I'm tired of it."

"I understand."

"You do?"

Michael let his measuring tape roll back into its case with a snap. "Do you have any idea how many Michaels and Mikes there are around here? Amish ones and Mennonite ones and *Englisch* ones and lots of other ones. Every day I hear someone use my name, but they aren't talking to me. They're talking to someone else."

"Don't you hate it, too?"

Michael shook his head and gave the boy a gentle smile. "Not any longer. It used to annoy me, but I realized it was such a *wunderbaar* name it needed to be given to many different people. My twin brother's name is Gabriel, and I know only one other person with his name. He used to say, when we were kids, he wished he could have a friend with the same name like I did."

"Not me. I wish I could change my name. It's not unusual for people to do that, y'know?"

"Who do you know who's changed his name?"

"My mom. Her name wasn't always Carolyn Wiebe. It was something different. If she can do it, why can't I?"

He tried not to laugh at the boy's sense of unfairness in his situation. Of course, Carolyn would have changed her name after she married. All plain women did.

But why did she never talk about the man she'd wed? Could something have happened, something that caused the shadows in her eyes? She held on to secrets of her past as tightly as she did the *kinder*. He wasn't sure where she'd moved from. She'd mentioned an older sister, but then changed the subject so fast he'd nearly gotten whiplash.

She's wiser than you, taunted a small voice in his mind. *She's put her past to rest while you let yours dog your every step through life.*

He halted the saw in midcut. He'd never looked at the situation from that angle.

"Are you okay, Michael?" asked the *kind*.

"I'm fine. Just fine."

He distracted the boy and himself by building a door to set into the doorway he'd cut. When it became too dark to work any longer, he took Kevin to the community center.

He opened the door and saw Carolyn on the other side of the long room with Jenna and Abby. Her sweet laughter drifted across the room to him, enthralling him in its lyrical song. He thought they were sharing a joke, and then Jenna stepped aside. On the floor, two pies were smashed to pieces.

"It's all right," Carolyn was reassuring her friend. "We can make more pies. Jose has made sure we've got plenty of apples."

"But," Jenna moaned, "look at the time we've lost. How can we make more pies and have time to do everything else?"

Abby glanced at the clock. "It's getting late, and we need to finish preparing the evening meal before everyone gets here."

Unperturbed by either the pie filling oozing across the floor or her friends' despondent tones, Carolyn said, "We've got enough time if we get started now. Once we get this cleaned up, Abby, you can start making more crusts while Jenna and I peel and cut the apples."

None of the women looked at Michael as they hurried into the kitchen. It was for the best, because his face must have displayed his admiration for how Carolyn handled any crisis, no matter how big or small. He couldn't imagine her making a mockery of someone else to turn all eyes to her.

Michael closed the door, backed away and walked down the hill. He paused by the brook and switched on his flashlight. It shocked him how such an innocuous trickle had caused the damage he'd seen in the village. The soft whisper of the water flowing over the stones was almost lost in the sound of voices coming from his right. He saw the lights were on in the diner by the road over the bridge. The owners must be working so they could open after the first of the year as they'd announced.

Though they were busy with their own work and hadn't seen him by the brook, he continued downstream. He had a lot to think about tonight, but most especially he needed to decide if he should make the change in his future that would allow him to pose an offer of marriage to Carolyn.

Though she wondered why Michael hadn't come in when he'd brought Kevin, Carolyn didn't have time to find out. After she helped with the pies to replace the ones that had slid off Jenna's tray, she made batch after batch of brownies for the workers who were coming in to get their suppers. The cold seemed to make everyone ravenous.

"Why the long face?" Jenna asked as she came into the community kitchen. With the pies baking in the large ovens, she'd regained her good spirits.

"Brownies used to be one of my favorite treats." Carolyn glowered at the bowl in front of her. "But after stirring my tenth batch today, I'm not sure I ever want to smell one again."

Jenna dipped her finger into the bowl and licked it. "Ah, chocolate! One of God's best creations." She reached for an apron from the stack on the counter. She pulled out one in shades of bright red and green and tied it around her. "I know you like chocolate as much as I do, so stop grousing. You'll be at the front of the line anytime someone is passing out warm brownies."

"How's Benjamin doing at the library?"

"Helpful, but impatient to get back to working on the houses. Kind of like Rose Anne, but larger." She laughed as she reached for a bag of dried bread and began to cut it into cubes for the stuffing they needed to make before they left tonight. "He wants to do everything he usually does, but then gets a reminder he shouldn't."

"Rose Anne hasn't slowed down much. When I checked on her last night, I found she'd climbed into Kevin's bed so she could sleep with him."

"With a cast on?" Jenna smiled. "Ah, to be young and unaware of what you should and shouldn't be able to do with a broken arm."

The sound of the back door opening was accompanied by a whoosh of air so cold it conquered the hot kitchen. At the call of her name, Carolyn whirled to see Michael slipping in. He closed the door and pulled off his scarf, then motioned for her to come over to where he stood.

"Why are you coming in the back way?" she asked.

"Hurry!"

She glanced at Jenna, who shrugged. Walking toward him, she said nothing as he looked around as if to determine who else was in the kitchen.

"What's going on?" she asked.

He put a paper bag on the floor, and she heard something rustle inside as it settled to the bottom. As he began to unbutton his coat, he said, "I didn't want Kevin to see me until I had a chance to talk to you first."

"Why?"

"Because I wanted you to see what I've got before he does."

Every word he spoke confused her more. "Michael, if this is your idea of a joke, it's not—"

"Look." He grabbed the bag and thrust his hand into it.

She gasped when she stared at what she'd never expected to see again. The tattered toy had been stained by mud and debris, but she recognized the floppy ears and the once-bushy tail, though it was almost two inches shorter than it had been. Her fingers quivered as she reached to take it from his icy fingers. The toy was damp, but not soaked. Turning it over, she saw the spot where she'd stitched a rip closed last summer.

He whispered, "Is it Tippy?"

Unable to speak as tears rushed into her eyes, she nodded. She cleared her throat once, then a second time before she could ask, "Where did you find him? *How* did you find him?"

"The how part was simple. I stumbled over it while I was walking along the brook tonight."

Her head snapped up. "You were walking along the brook in the cold and dark? Have you lost your mind?"

"I needed to sort out some important things, and walking always helps me do that."

"And you found Tippy?" She ran the back of her hand under her eyes to dash away the tears that refused to stay put. "Where?"

"Down along the curve of the brook. There's a car

stuck on the bank." He sighed. "I think it's yours. It's black. Both the front lights and the rear ones are shattered, and there are small rocks behind the portions of the intact glass. I waded out into the brook to see if the license plate was on it. When I was bending down to aim my flashlight at the front, I saw something stuck among the torn plants and small trees embedded in the space between the bumper and the radiator. I was curious because it was above the water."

"Tippy," she whispered, unable to believe what she held in her hands.

"I wasn't sure if it was Kevin's, but I figured I'd bring it back here. If it wasn't his, some other kid would be looking for it."

"It's his. God put you in the right place at the right time."

"Me and Tippy."

"Yes, both of you were in the right place at the right time to find each other." She brushed the ruffled fur back into place, then reached out and grabbed Michael's hand.

He chuckled as she pulled him into the other room. Did he think she cared if everyone in Evergreen Corners saw her holding his hand now? She didn't slow until she reached the corner where Kevin was helping his sister choose a crayon out of a big plastic box. She pushed the stuffed dog back into Michael's hands. He'd recovered it, so he should be the one to give it to her nephew.

"Kevin," she said in a shaky voice.

Both *kinder* looked up at the same time.

"Michael has something for you," she went on, stepping aside.

Holding out the battered toy, Michael said, "Here's someone who's been missing you."

Kevin jumped to his feet and cried out his toy's name. He snatched the stuffed dog from Michael's hands and stared at it, then he looked at her. When she nodded, he pressed the dog to his chest. With his cheek against the dog's head, he began to sob as he folded to sit on the floor.

She knelt and put her arm around him. Seeing his sister ease closer, she drew the little girl within the arc of her arm, too. She took Michael's hand. There were no words to thank him, so she didn't try.

He gazed at her with tears in his own eyes. No one else moved as her nephew welcomed home a dear friend he'd thought was lost forever.

Suddenly, a timer went off in the kitchen, and the world flowed into motion again as the bakers rushed out and conversations began everywhere.

Everywhere but where she held her children and the hand of the man she wanted to love. Could she put aside her trepidation and dare to trust him with her heart?

She had from now until year's end to find out. Not only if she could trust him with her heart, but if she could trust her heart itself.

Chapter Thirteen

The last thing Carolyn expected was for Michael to stop at the trailer at dawn on Thanksgiving morning. The children were in her bedroom watching Tippy roll over and over in the dryer. Though she'd been anxious the toy would fall apart when she washed it, the stuffed dog had come through its bath looking almost as it had before. Kevin had discovered one of its eyes was missing, and Carolyn had promised to sew on a new one as soon as they could buy a button.

"Do Mennonites have Christmas trees?" Michael asked as he poked his head past the door.

She didn't glance up from the German chocolate cake she was frosting. It felt wonderful to be baking again. She'd finally mastered the quirks of the trailer's oven and now was able to make sponge cakes and bundt cakes and coffeecakes. She'd forgotten how much she missed putting gooey dough into an oven and a short time later pulling out aromatic, spongy cake layers. Too much else had been on her mind, but mixing the ingredients and enjoying the results had kept her focused instead of anxious as it had ever since...

Since she'd left Indiana with the children.

Propelling that thought into the back of her mind, she was able to smile as she motioned for Michael to come in. His kindness during the past month was one of the reasons she felt a contentment she'd thought she'd never experience again. She had spent half the night awake as she sought the right words to thank him for bringing Tippy back to Kevin. Everything she thought of seemed too vapid to convey the depths of her appreciation.

"Christmas trees?" she asked. "It's almost a month before we celebrate Christmas. Why are you asking?"

"But do you Mennonites have Christmas trees?" He came in and closed the door.

The small trailer seemed to shrink more as his broad shoulders and vital personality filled the space. She gave herself a moment to savor the sight of his strong features. A quiver ran from her heart right to the tips of her toes as she recalled his hand holding hers the previous night. Yes, she'd grabbed his first when she dragged him into the main room, but he hadn't released her fingers until she had to return to work on the feast for this afternoon.

Despite her heart urging her to believe he was the man he appeared to be, she had to select her words with care. It was the same walk across a tightrope she'd been doing for four years. She wouldn't lie, but she had to avoid spilling the truth that could lead to a disaster greater than the flood.

"Some Mennonite families have trees," she replied, applying more coconut-pecan icing to the cake. "Some don't. It depends on how conservative a family's beliefs are or what their traditions are. Sometimes the differences range from family to family rather than from district to district as with you Amish."

He pulled off his black felt hat and brushed his too-long hair back from his eyes. The man needed a haircut. Should she offer? That was the job of an Amish woman. Maybe she should suggest to Abby that it was time for the plain men to have their hair trimmed.

"I guess I should have asked if *your* family has a Christmas tree," he said.

"We do."

She had relented and gotten Kevin and Rose Anne a tree their first year in Evergreen Corners. In part, it'd been so their house didn't stand out as the one without a tree. But the main reason she had given in was that her sister had put up a small tree every year because she'd lived an *Englisch* life, and Kevin had faint memories of those. Decorating the tree with popcorn strings and hand-made ornaments and not putting on lights had eased Carolyn's regret about another sign of how far she'd moved from the life she'd known.

The life she'd always expected to live.

The life you could have again if you told Michael the truth and he became part of the family.

She silenced the thought. Going to live in an Amish community could give Leland the lead he needed to find them.

"Why are you asking?" she asked.

He grinned, and she looked at the cake before she couldn't resist his smile and grabbed his hand again. This time to pull it around her waist as she stepped into his arms.

"*Englischers* seem to have a tradition," he explained, "of putting a Christmas tree on top of any building project in progress at this time of year."

"On the roof?"

"*Ja.*"

"So you're going to put a Christmas tree on top of the brand-new shingles on my roof?"

He smiled and leaned a shoulder against the upper cabinets. As before, she was astonished by how little space there was between his shoulders and the cupboards on either side of the tiny kitchen. "I had the same thought, Carolyn. I was told, in this case, the trees would be put in front of the houses, so they could be seen from the road." His smile faded. "The other two houses belong to *Englischers*, and they're thrilled with the idea. I wanted to check to make sure you're okay with it, too."

"The children will be excited about it." She hedged, hoping it was enough of an answer.

It wasn't, because he asked, "How do *you* feel about it?"

"I'm grateful for what you are doing for us. I wouldn't care if you wanted to put a dancing elephant in front of the house." She wagged a finger. "But no elephant on the roof."

He caught her finger in his broad hand, then ran his finger along hers, catching the frosting on his rougher skin. Popping the frosting into his mouth, he gave her a slow, enticing smile. "Delicious."

The familiar frisson rippled through her center, but she laughed to break the invisible connection between them. "You sound like the kids when they plead to lick the spoon."

"Some things a guy shouldn't grow too old to try. Baseball, horseshoes and beguiling frosting or raw cookie dough from a skilled baker."

She scooped out a generous spoonful of the icing that was as rich as fudge and offered it to him. "Here you go."

"Me, too?" asked Rose Anne from behind her as she and Kevin rushed from the bedroom. "Can I have some?"

"Can I have *lots*?" chimed in her brother.

As she handed each child a small taste of the frosting, Rose Anne asked, "Sit with us at supper, Michael, okay?"

"That's the best invitation I've had all day," he replied. "As long as it's okay with your *mamm*."

"Of course it is." Carolyn was glad her voice didn't convey the excitement going off in her like a fireworks show finale. Michael would have Thanksgiving with them. *Like a real family.*

Oh, how she wished that was possible, but no matter how much her heart begged her to give it to Michael, she must keep the children safe.

She was relieved she didn't have to say more before Michael headed out and the children returned to the bedroom to watch Tippy's wild journey around the dryer. When she was alone again in the kitchen, she took a deep breath, wondering when she'd last drawn a steady one. Not since she'd heard Michael's voice as he came into the trailer.

Her fingers tightened around the spoon until the wood creaked. Loosening her grip, she drew in another slow breath. All she had to do was keep her heart under control until Michael returned to his brother's farm.

Opening the door to the community center, Michael smiled. The place was bustling as church members and other villagers, including the mayor and most of her council, joined the volunteers for a Thanksgiving meal. It was made up of dishes from the many different groups in the room. Amish noodles and chow-chow were set on the table beside Mennonite dishes that ranged from brimming casseroles topped with crispy browned cheese to a pear and walnut salad drizzled with maple syrup. Homemade breads from white to pumpernickel were displayed with sweet rolls in baskets along the long tables set in a giant U in the center of the room. Potatoes and yams and green beans had been placed in the centers of the tables while butternut soup had been ladled into bowls on top of each plate.

He looked forward to sampling, but most of all he wanted a piece of the German chocolate cake Carolyn had been frosting a few hours ago. Its aroma had been astounding, and the frosting the best he'd ever tasted. He wanted to try both together. However, first there was the meal to consider.

"Nobody's going to go away hungry," Benjamin said as he struggled to get his coat off so he could toss it atop the others piled on chairs by the front door.

Michael almost offered his help, but knew his friend would turn him down. Benjamin was determined to be able to return to doing everything he could before the accident…even if his mulishness injured his healing ribs more.

Shouts came for everyone to take a seat. Michael hurried to where Kevin and Rose Anne sat with Jenna's daughter, Taylor. Streaks of red on the festive tablecloth announced little fingers had already been in the cranberry sauce.

Cheers broke out just as Michael sat, leaving one empty chair between himself and Kevin. Benjamin gave him a grin, then chose the seat on Michael's other side. The cheers became applause as the stars of the day arrived in the common room. Not the six women who'd been working in the kitchen, but the turkeys they carried on large platters. Abby led the way, holding up a perfectly cooked bird.

"That one's as big as me," Rose Anne said loudly.

Her words brought more cheers as well as convivial laughter.

"Then it should go right by you." Jenna put the turkey she'd brought beside where Rose Anne and Taylor sat.

After placing the turkey she'd brought out in front of Pastor Hershey, Carolyn hurried to the empty chair between Kevin and Michael. She smiled at him, but looked down the table as the Mennonite minister rose.

The room hushed while Pastor Hershey asked each person to thank God for His blessings in his or her own way. Soft prayers flowed through the room like a breeze on a perfect summer day, though the Amish were silent. When the minister said, "Amen," every head rose and silverware clicked as they began to enjoy the soup.

Jenna smiled along the table. "When I was growing up, we'd say what we were thankful for. Michael, why don't you start?"

He was surprised she didn't ask Benjamin first, but said, "I've got many reasons to be thankful this Thanksgiving. My brother is happily married and has the farm he's wanted since we were kids. I'm getting ready to do the work I love in what will be three *wunderbaar* homes. And I'm blessed with many new friends."

He watched Carolyn's face while he spoke. Did she have any idea *she* was what he was most thankful for this year?

Kevin was next. "I'm thankful Michael brought Tippy home," the boy announced, and smiles along the table broadened.

Carolyn spoke of her gratitude for the volunteers who'd come to Evergreen Corners. "And, as Michael said, you've become our friends."

Everyone's smiles widened more when Rose Anne announced she was grateful for the pies waiting to be served for dessert.

"Which is your favorite?" Benjamin asked.

"Pun-kin." Rose Anne giggled as she added, "I'm going to have a big piece with whip-it cream on it."

"Whippet?" asked Michael as he leaned toward Carolyn. "I hope you aren't putting small greyhounds on top of the pies."

"I wasn't planning on it." She spooned some mashed potatoes onto Rose Anne's plate before stretching to do the same for Kevin. She gave him another half spoonful when he offered her a mournful glance. "I figured I'd use regular whipped cream."

"Sounds delicious."

"But no dessert for anyone who doesn't finish their supper," she said as she aimed the same unrelenting frown at her daughter and her son and then on to him.

That she included him brought peals of laughter from her children and Jenna's daughter. As others spoke of why they were blessed, Michael let himself relish the merriment and the gratitude. Now was the time for feasting and laughing and sharing each other's company.

There was time enough later to speak to her about what he'd decided as he walked by the brook.

Carolyn rearranged the trailer's small refrigerator for the third time and managed to squeeze in the two servings of green bean casserole Jenna had insisted she bring home with her. Straightening, she sighed. It had been a good day, but a long one. She was glad they could live on leftovers for the next few meals. She picked up her cup of tea and carried it to the table where Michael sat nursing the decaf coffee he'd made while she got the children into bed.

Checking both children, she saw they were asleep.

She sighed again, this time with happiness, at the sight of Kevin lying with his cheek on Tippy.

"Can I get your opinion about something important?" Michael asked when she put her cup on the table.

"Of course."

She slid into the banquette across from him. Her joy tempered when she noticed his fingers tapping the table. What was he nervous about? "Do I need to make some decision about the house?"

"No, nothing about the house or the *kinder* or you." He paused, and his gaze slid away from hers as if he were ashamed of what he was about to say.

She couldn't imagine what it might be. He was a good man, the best she'd ever met. Putting a gentle hand on his arm, she said, "Tell me."

"I'm not sure I want to be baptized Amish."

She was struck speechless by his words. Not be baptized Amish? Did he have any idea of what he would lose if he decided not to become a part of the *Leit* in Harmony Creek Hollow? Images of her past, spending time with neighbors and friends who offered her an escape from the cruel words in her house, zoomed out of her memories. The love and acceptance of her plain community had been the bulwark God had offered her against the secrets hidden behind the Hilty family's walls. She should tell Michael how much she missed those connections and that community.

But she couldn't.

She bit her lower lip and stared at her clenched fingers laced together on the table. When she'd embarked on the path she was sure God had set out for her, she'd never imagined she'd come to such an impossible crossroads. She ached to trust Michael, but feared sharing her secret with anyone risked the truth leaking out to the whole world.

Including Leland.

She ached to speak from the heart, but pushed aside her own pain as she thought of what she might call down upon the children.

"It must be a big decision." She loathed herself as soon as the platitude came out of her mouth. Michael was hurting as he sought the path God had created for him. Instead of comforting him, she was offering him a useless cliché.

"A huge one." He sighed.

"Are you unhappy with your Amish community?" If she kept him talking, she might find a roundabout way to help him, a way that didn't endanger the children.

"No." He folded his hands in front of him. "My twin brother and his family are part of it. So are James and Benjamin. Our neighbors made us feel welcome from the day we arrived in Harmony Creek Hollow."

"It sounds like a lovely place."

"It is." He gave her a lopsided grin. "In fact, Evergreen Corners reminds me a lot of it. You may not be Amish, but the people here are a community that cares for one another. In the month since the flood, nobody has backed away from offering to help."

"But if you're happy there, is it because you question your faith?"

"Who hasn't questioned their faith at one time or another? That's part of the weakness of being human. I'm thankful God is patient enough to keep loving me as a *kind* who has much to learn and accept and rejoice in."

"Then why…?" She wasn't sure what else to ask.

"Once I'm baptized, I'll be expected to find an Amish girl to marry, so we can raise a family in our faith traditions. Marrying someone outside our faith would mean being put under the *bann*."

She stared at him, her mouth agape. He couldn't be thinking of putting off being baptized because of any feelings he had for *her*, could he? Her heart sank. If he was making his choice because of her, he was making it without knowing the truth. How could she let him make such a life-altering decision while she withheld information from him?

But she couldn't tell him the truth.

Nothing had changed, she realized. It wouldn't until Rose Anne and Kevin were old enough to understand why she'd taken them from their home in Indiana and brought them to Vermont.

Wanting to hear him say he loved her as she loved him, she knew she must set aside that dream as she had others. She couldn't let him give up the life he knew and the family he loved based on what he believed she was.

But she couldn't tell him the truth.

"If you want my advice, Michael, don't make your decision now," she said, hoping to calm her roiling stomach. "At least, not while you're in Evergreen Corners."

His breath sifted past his clenched teeth, and she got the feeling she'd missed something. Something he hadn't said, but had wanted her to know.

"Take the time," she urged him, "to pray on it and see what guidance God offers you. He knows what you should do, but He may not let you know until His time is right."

"Rather than my own timetable, you mean?"

She nodded, biting back her own answer. If she said *ja* now, he might think she was making fun of his way of talking. She didn't want him to think that, and she couldn't explain how tough it was to avoid slipping into *Deitsch* when they spoke of their faith.

"That's *gut* advice." He gave her a rigid smile, then set himself on his feet. "*Danki* for listening, Carolyn. I appreciate the perspective of someone who's not Amish. You're right. This is between me and God and will be resolved at the time He deems right."

Her heart didn't know whether to jump in celebration that he was going to make his decision through prayer and patience or whether it should tumble in despair that he considered her an outsider not involved in his life.

And why shouldn't he? demanded the logical part of her brain. *He doesn't know you were raised Amish.*

"I know you'll make the best decision," she said, again falling back on the trite.

"If I heed God's guidance, I will." He cupped her cheek.

She yearned to lean her head into his strong, work-hardened palm and tell him how she longed for his arms around her again, how she wanted to share the secrets stalking her, how she wished she could tell him about her heart dancing with joy whenever she saw him or heard his voice. She didn't say anything.

"Gut nacht," he said as he pulled on his coat and reached for his hat, which he'd left by the sink.

"Good night," she whispered, but he was already gone.

She went to the door and looked out the small window. She watched him fade into the darkness. She stood there for uncounted minutes, turning only when she heard Rose Anne give a half sob. Going to check her niece, she ignored the tears running down her own face as she wondered if, somewhere, Leland Reber was laughing at how he'd ruined her life, too.

Chapter Fourteen

$\mathcal{A}$s he walked across the village green, Michael scratched his nape beneath his wool coat. It was always itchy in the wake of getting his hair cut. He should have been grateful Abby had come to the community center with her scissors and a battery-powered razor to give the plain men the opportunity to have their hair trimmed. He wasn't the only one who'd gotten tired of hair falling into his eyes when he bent to drive a nail or measure a length of wood. There had been seven men standing in line when he got there. Piles of hair in every possible shade had littered the floor.

Looking at the boy beside him, Michael smiled. Kevin had insisted on getting his hair cut, too, because he'd declared himself a full member of the volunteers. Carolyn had given her permission, so Michael had put Kevin in front of him in the line.

Carolyn was an excellent *mamm*, stern when she needed to be but willing to let her *kinder* make choices when she could. He'd seen her glance at little *bopplin*, and he guessed she wanted more *kinder*, though she'd shown no particular interest in any of the bachelors in the Mennonite community.

Or any interest in him, according to her response on Thanksgiving night when he'd opened up to her about his uncertainty regarding baptism. She'd given him every argument to become a member of the Harmony Creek Hollow *Leit*. Or, as she'd said more than once, he should let God guide him and not hurry the decision.

Those were the exact words he'd debated with himself about for months. If he'd sought his twin's advice, he would have expected Gabriel to make almost identical suggestions. Eli, the district's minister, wouldn't have told him anything else, and if his *daed* were still living, he'd have advised Michael the same way.

But he'd hoped for something more from a woman he'd been ready to propose to. A woman who seemed to be what he wanted as a wife. Had he been wrong about the light sparkling in her eyes when she looked at him? He didn't want to think so, but he'd been wrong about Adah.

Somehow, he'd let more than three weeks pass without talking to Carolyn about anything else important. He kept telling himself he'd speak to her about his feelings... tomorrow. Not that he had much time because she'd been busy with the *kinder* and village events for Christmas. He'd been as absorbed working on the houses, even being drafted to go with Glen and Jose twice to get supplies in Massachusetts.

Excuses, he told himself as he had before.

Now, as he walked through the biting cold with Kevin, he knew he couldn't put off being honest with her. He was scheduled to finish his volunteer stint in ten days.

"It's Christmas Eve eve," the boy said, as if Michael had been sharing his uneasy thoughts.

"That's right." He made himself chuckle. "So that makes yesterday Christmas Eve eve eve, ain't so?"

"Don't be silly!" Kevin rolled his eyes with a skill he'd likely hone further as a teenager. "There's no such thing!"

"I'm glad I've got you around, buddy, to keep me straight on things."

"So why don't you stay around?"

"I'm not sure what you mean."

"I mean why don't you stay here instead of going back to Harmony Creek Hollow?"

"My family is there."

"Your family could be here," Kevin said with the certainty of a *kind*.

He shook his head. "My brother won't want to move away because he can't wait to get working his fields this spring. You should come to Harmony Creek Hollow. You could visit Gabriel's cows and his wife Leanna's goats."

"Goats?" Kevin grimaced. "Don't they eat your clothes?"

"Only if you're *dumm* enough to leave them in a pile in their pen."

"I don't think I'd like goats."

"Maybe you'd like the soap Leanna makes out of their milk."

"Ugh!"

Michael swallowed his chuckle. He wasn't sure if Kevin was disgusted at the idea of goat milk soap or soap in general. "You might change your mind if you came to visit."

"I know what you should do," Kevin said as if Michael hadn't spoken.

"Do you?" He nodded to a bundled-up man walking across the green.

He wasn't sure who it was, now that many of the *Englischers* were growing beards for the winter. The man hurried past them without speaking. Michael didn't blame him. The wind seemed to be getting more frigid by the second.

"Yep, I do!" Kevin didn't seem bothered by the cold as he turned and faced him. "I know what you should do."

"What's that?"

"You should marry Mommy, and then you could be my uncle."

A buzzing had erupted in Michael's head when Kevin said "marry" and "Mommy" in the same breath. That had to be why he'd misunderstood the rest of the boy's words.

"You mean your *daed*, ain't so?"

Kevin's grin grew so wide it almost escaped his face. "Yes, you can be my daddy-uncle. Like Mommy is my mommy-aunt."

He didn't want to insult the boy by saying Kevin was confused. Or was he? Kevin was an intelligent *kind* with an agile mind and a vocabulary far beyond other boys his age.

"What's a mommy-aunt?" he asked.

"Guess it should be aunt-mommy. See, first she was my aunt and then she became my mommy after my other mommy died."

Every word the boy spoke made more questions blossom in Michael's head. Asking Kevin wouldn't get him anywhere. He needed Carolyn to explain. It was long past time to learn about the past she'd been hiding from him.

Putting the last cookie sheet away in the drawer under the stove, Carolyn closed it quietly. She didn't want to wake Rose Anne, who was napping on the narrow sofa. The thought of taking a nap gave birth to a big yawn. She surrendered to it, hoping letting it escape would leave her with enough energy to mop the floor before she began supper.

Twelve dozen cookies.

A gross of chocolate chip cookies and snickerdoodles and oatmeal raisin nut cookies were packaged and waiting to go to the community center tomorrow. They'd be served at the Christmas Eve caroling on the green. She'd been so pleased to be asked to contribute, though it had been a challenge to mix, bake and store so many cookies in the cramped kitchen.

She glanced out the window. Michael should be bringing Kevin back soon. They'd been gone almost two hours, and the line for haircuts couldn't have been too long. There were fewer than a dozen Amish men in town.

Her smile returned when she remembered how Kevin had taken his pocketknife with him so Michael could show him more tricks to whittling. Her nephew was eager to learn, and there wasn't room in the trailer. With the arrival of winter two days ago, it was too cold for them to sit on the steps.

Maybe in the spring…

Her breath caught when she remembered that by spring, Michael would be living in Harmony Creek Hollow over fifty miles away. She didn't want to think about a time when he wouldn't be close by.

A knock on the trailer door made her square her shoulders and paste on a smile. She opened the door and started to speak. She paused when she saw Benjamin standing beside Michael and Kevin.

"What a nice surprise, Benjamin!" she said. "Come in."

"Carolyn, will you get your coat and take a walk with me?" Michael asked, his voice so serious she gripped the edge of the door frame. "Benjamin will watch the *kinder* for you."

Looking from one man to the other, she nodded. What was going? She rushed to get her coat, hat and gloves. Pulling them on, she slipped past where Benjamin was edging to sit at the table. She invited him to try any of the cookies still on the counter.

"The ones on the trays are for tomorrow night," she said. "There's coffee and—"

"We'll be fine." Benjamin smiled. "Enjoy your walk."

She realized the circumstances couldn't be so serious if Michael's friend was grinning. Pausing only to tell Kevin his haircut looked good, she went out to where Michael stood with his gloved hands beneath his folded arms.

She wasn't surprised when they walked toward her new home, but she was shocked Michael said nothing. The silence pressed on them, and the sound of children playing football on the other side of the green barely intruded. She wasn't accustomed to feeling uncomfortable with Michael, but she sensed he had something important on his mind.

Will he tell me he loves me? She had to keep herself from twirling around like Rose Anne at the thrilling thought. If that was what he wanted to talk to her about when they were walking out together—she tried not to laugh at the thought of the Amish words for courting—she must not rush him. Hearing him speak from the heart would be worth every second she had to wait.

When he paused outside the library that was a dark hulk as the sun sank behind the mountains, he asked, "Why does Kevin call you his mommy-aunt?"

She put her fingers to her lips, but her gasp escaped.

She'd thought Kevin had forgotten the phrase he'd used right after she brought the children to Vermont.

"Because it's the truth." Saying the words was a relief as she put down a huge burden she'd been carrying too long.

"You can't be both his *mamm* and his *aenti*."

"But I am."

"He said he had another *mamm*. Is that true?"

She motioned toward the steps. "You should sit because this is a long story." She gave a terse laugh. "Actually, it isn't that long, though it felt like forever when we were living it."

He didn't move, so she launched into how Leland Reber's cruelty to Regina had led to Carolyn leaving Indiana with the children and moving to Evergreen Corners after her sister's death. She didn't downplay her fear or how she doubted the court granting her custody of her niece and nephew would have done anything to protect them from their father.

"So you lived in a Mennonite community in Indiana?" he asked.

Closing her eyes, she prayed God would give her strength to say what she must and that He'd open Michael's ears and his heart to listening to her. She looked at him and said, "No, I lived in the Amish district where I was born."

"You're Amish?"

She nodded, dropping her gaze because she couldn't bear to see what was in his.

"So everything I know about you is a lie?"

She recoiled from his harsh tone. "The only things I changed were our names and the children's ages."

"Kinder." The single word was clipped as if he'd cut it in half with a circular saw.

"What?"

"You might as well use the *Deitsch* words," he said in the language of her childhood. "I know you understand them."

"I do." She wished he hadn't switched to *Deitsch*. For her, the language of the Amish should draw people together rather than tear them apart. "I tried to be careful, but I know I made mistakes."

"You did." He shifted to look at the library. "So did I."

She ached to tear down the walls he was building between them, moving farther from her than he'd ever been. "What would you have done if you were in my situation?"

"I would have sought help from the *Leit*."

"And what *gut* would that have done if Leland had come to demand I turn Kevin and Rose Anne over to him in spite of me having legal custody?"

"Then you could have contacted the police."

She clamped her arms together in front of her. "Nobody in our district would have gone to the *Englisch* authorities without talking first to our bishop."

"Then you should have gone to your bishop."

"I couldn't. He's Leland's great-uncle and was fixated on Leland coming back and being baptized." She shook her head. "Maybe the bishop could have forgiven him for putting my sister in the hospital more than once with his abuse, but I couldn't." She blinked back tears. "You don't know how many times I tried, Michael, but I can't. And maybe that's why it's best I left my *Leit*. How can I be Amish when I can't forgive Leland or myself?"

She didn't give him a chance to answer. Instead, she

raced away across the green toward the sanctuary of her trailer, dragging her ragged hopes with her.

Christmas Eve dawned with lazy snowflakes falling beyond the stable windows. Like the cards Michael had seen in the project office, the scene of great pine trees frosted with fresh snow seemed the perfect setting for celebrations of the Christ Child's birth. The snow on the mountains glistened in the subdued sunlight sifting through the clouds, but a sparse inch of snow perched atop the grass and leaves. It should have imbued the view with happy anticipation of the holidays.

Instead, all he felt was disbelief. Carolyn had been false with him. Just as Adah had been. Though she hadn't tossed him aside spectacularly, she'd listened to the troubles of his heart and never once admitted she'd had to make a decision herself to stay among the Amish or leave. *Ja*, the circumstances were different, but he'd given her the opportunity to be honest with him on Thanksgiving night.

He swung his feet over the side of his cot, but didn't stand. Cold crawled up his legs. He should shove his feet into the slippers he'd been given after he moved into the stables.

He didn't.

He sat and stared at the floor. It should have been covered by hay and bits of oats dropped when the horse that lived in the stall was eating. And he should be somewhere else.

Where?

He didn't know where he should be, but coming to Evergreen Corners had been a mistake. No, that had been fine. He shouldn't have gotten involved with Carolyn and her family. Why was he tempted to laugh when there wasn't anything funny about the blunder he'd made when he thought she was as averse to drama as he was?

She was a walking, talking bundle of drama.

Everything he told himself he didn't want in his life. Wasn't that so?

He put his head in his hands and tried to pray, but he wasn't sure what he wanted to ask God for. To harden his heart so it didn't ache? No, he didn't want that.

"Gute mariye," came Benjamin's voice from the other side of the stall. The wall between them creaked, and Michael knew his friend had folded his arms on top of it. "Late night last night?" When Michael didn't answer, he went on, "You look like you've been run over by one of the big excavators. Twice."

Michael raised his head, but didn't bother to try to smile at Benjamin's teasing. Nor did he explain to his friend how he'd spent the night tossing and turning, unable to sleep. He hadn't kept Benjamin awake, because a steady snoring had come from the other stall throughout the night while Michael waited for the darkness to thin into the first cold light of dawn.

"Trouble sleeping," he admitted, hoping if he did then his friend would let the matter go.

Benjamin didn't. "Did you and Carolyn have an argument?"

"Why would you ask such a thing?"

He shrugged. "I can't think of any other reason why she came back to the trailer alone and looked as if she was trying not to cry. I waited for you to say something last evening, but you stomped around like you wanted to drive your boots a foot deep into the ground."

Standing and reaching for his work clothes, Michael said, "I'm confused. That's all."

"About how you feel about Carolyn? Because let me tell you, if you're confused, you're the only one. Everyone else can see how much you care about her and the *kinder*. Then why—?"

Michael aimed a quick prayer of gratitude up to God when Benjamin was called away by one of the other volunteers now sharing the stable. He regretted such an insensitive prayer. Benjamin was trying to cheer him, but repairing a broken heart was a much tougher task than building a house.

And he knew it would take much, much longer.

Chapter Fifteen

"Mommy, what's wrong?" Rose Anne leaned against Carolyn's leg as they found a place among the villagers on the green. The Christmas Eve concert was being performed by the unified choirs from several churches in the village in front of the still unrepaired gazebo. Light from the waning moon, not much more than a slender crescent, shone down on the gathering.

"Nothing you need to worry about, sweetheart." She ruffled the little girl's soft curls that refused to stay beneath her cap and made sure the knit band covered her niece's ears. The temperature was going down fast, though the air remained dank with the odor of snow.

"But you look sad, and that makes me sad."

"Me, too." Kevin pushed his hands into his pockets, standing stiff, a sure sign he was upset.

Her heart filled more at their concern for her. Forcing a smile onto her lips, she bent toward them. "I've got a lot on my mind. So many decisions to make about the house."

Both statements were true, but neither spoke of the

pain clamped around her heart because she'd refused to admit another truth.

Not to others this time, but to herself.

She loved her niece and nephew with her whole heart, but she wanted her heart to belong to Michael Miller. So many fantasies she'd created, dreaming he might love her, too. She'd imagined him coming in his mud-stained work clothes and boots to propose. She'd thought of him asking her to be his wife while he wore his *mutze* coat and vest. The same clothes he'd be wearing when they stood side by side in front of the ministers and bishop marrying them.

What a mess she'd made of everything! But she couldn't imagine anything she could have done differently. She'd have had to tell him the truth sometime. She'd planned to when...

She flinched at the realization she'd never given thought to choosing the best time to tell him about why she and the children were in Evergreen Corners. But she'd intended to tell him.

Hadn't she?

Listening to the choir begin "Joy to the World," she wrapped her arms around herself. She couldn't hold the cold out when it gnawed deep within her heart. She had fallen in love with Michael, but hadn't been ready to trust him. The legacy of secrets and abuse she'd witnessed prevented that.

"Mommy!" Rose Anne tugged on her coat.

"Yes?" she asked beneath the sweet, soaring notes.

"Can we go and see Taylor?"

Carolyn looked at where Jenna and her daughter were coming out of the community center. "All right. Don't cross the street."

"I know. I know. Stay on the green," Kevin said in a singsong voice.

Her aching heart lifted, or tried to, at her nephew using the tone of an adolescent who'd been reminded of a potential transgression too many times. She shooed them on their way and turned to watch the choir so she could avoid scanning the green to discover if Michael had joined the crowd.

"Mommy!" came a muffled cry that was abruptly cut off.

Carolyn stiffened. Rose Anne! She looked toward where her children had gone to meet Jenna. She saw her friend and Taylor, but not her nephew and niece.

Where were Kevin and Rose Anne?

She whirled to scan every direction across the snow-covered green. She couldn't see them anywhere.

Someone waved from the far side. The children! They weren't alone.

Who was with them?

She gasped when she saw a man had Rose Anne by the arm and was dragging her across the street. He stepped into the glow from a streetlight and glanced back at Kevin who was in pursuit. His face was illuminated as clearly as if he stood in sunshine.

Carolyn pressed her hands to her mouth to silence her scream, then began to run to stop him from taking her niece.

She'd never mistake that face and square jaw that had been visible in the bright light through his bushy beard.

Leland Reber!

People around Michael applauded as the choir finished the rollicking Christmas carol that was so different from the slow tempo of Amish hymns. The multipart harmony added both a lilt and a depth to the song unlike any he'd ever heard.

He'd come tonight at Benjamin's insistence. He hadn't wanted to stand in the cold with Carolyn a short distance away and try to act as if he weren't aware of everything she said and did. All day, she'd been on his mind. So much he'd pounded his thumb with a hammer, something he hadn't done since he first learned to drive nails. His hand throbbed, and his thumb was swollen to twice its normal size. He'd put some ice on it after supper at the community center, but its pain dimmed in comparison with the anguish searing him each time he thought about the grief and betrayal on Carolyn's face when she'd left him standing in front of the library last night.

Motion on the far side of the green, close to the main road and almost hidden by the tall pine tree beside the general store, caught his eye. He squinted, trying to bring the forms into focus. So many people had gathered on the green for the carol singing.

A faint cry teased his ears as the choir began their next song, but he recognized it. Kevin! The boy was calling out for help.

Help?

What was wrong?

His eyes widened when he saw Carolyn racing across the green. He yelled her name.

When she didn't stop, he started to shout after her again. He clamped his mouth closed when he heard her cry of horror.

"Leland, no! Don't take them!"

Her few words told him everything he needed to know. Leland Reber!

The *kinder*'s *daed*.

He was in Evergreen Corners?

No time for answers. He needed to get to Carolyn and the *kinder* before the man hurt them.

"Was iss letz?" asked Benjamin, reaching to grasp his arm.

With a quick sidestep, Michael eluded his friend's grip. He paid no attention to the shock on Benjamin's face. "I've got to go. They're in danger."

"Who?"

"Carolyn and the kids."

"What? Why?"

Another question Michael didn't respond to, though this time he knew the answer. Leland Reber! The man who'd been married to Carolyn's sister, the man who was the *kinder*'s *daed*. How had he found her and the *kinder*? More important, what was Leland going to do?

The answer came stark and appalling into his mind. To Benjamin he ordered, "Call 911! Now! Before he can hurt them more!"

As he gave chase, Michael heard his friend shouting for someone's cell phone.

The pounding of his boots on the ground echoed the name *Leland Reber*. He ran through a maze of people, all staring at him as if he'd lost his mind.

Slowing at the edge of the green, he looked in both directions. Where had they gone?

A childish shout came from the far side of the old mill in the center of the village. Was that one of Carolyn's *kinder* or someone else's?

He knew he couldn't wait to be sure. He had to take a chance. As he ran beside the three-story building, empty windows gave him no clue to what might be happening on the other side. He came around the end and stared down the steep bank toward where the brook was held back by the remnants of an old dam. Water rushed over it. If he shouted to Carolyn, she wouldn't hear him.

Ahead of him, a man with a bushy brown beard and mustache had Rose Anne under one arm. He was running toward the half-demolished covered bridge. Kevin was struggling to reach the man with Carolyn close behind.

He had no idea what Leland would do once he got to the bridge. Did the man know that route was cut off by damage from the flood? Would he turn like a trapped rat and attack? Leland had been raised plain, but Michael knew not everyone clung to the principles their elders tried to instill in them as *kinder*.

Then he saw a dark car waiting on the far side of the bridge. That must be where Leland was heading. The boards across the bridge were narrow, and he carried a struggling *kind*. Was the man crazy? If so, Carolyn was, as well, because she was closing the distance between them.

Spurring his own feet forward, Michael knew he wouldn't get to the bridge before Leland was on it. No matter. He had to stop the man from abducting Rose Anne.

Suddenly the bank dropped away. His feet slid out from under him, and he found himself sliding down the slope. Jamming his feet into the half-frozen ground, he kept himself from catapulting into the brook or over the dam. He pushed himself to his feet and groaned.

Not in pain, though he'd crushed his thumb against the hillside, but in horror as he watched Leland run across the pair of boards between the two open sections of the arches supporting the bridge. He held Rose Anne as if she were a bag of potatoes. Carolyn and Kevin were about to climb onto the bridge to follow him. Would the boards in the arch hold beneath them?

Save them, God. He didn't bother calling. Nothing would stop Carolyn or Kevin from trying to get Rose Anne back.

Carolyn screamed as Kevin wobbled beyond her outstretched arms.

Michael raced forward, though he was farther away. They couldn't let the boy fall twelve feet straight down into the stone-lined brook.

When Leland reached back and grabbed the boy, he yanked him toward the car. He held Kevin with one hand and shoved Rose Anne inside with the other. The little girl scrambled across the back seat and tried to open the other door. It wouldn't budge. She pounded on it with her tiny fists and shrieked in frustration.

"Stop!" Carolyn screamed.

Michael reached her in the shadows beneath the bridge's wrecked roof. "He's not going to listen. Stay here." He moved toward the man and the frightened *kinder*.

He doubted Carolyn would heed him. Nothing, not even her own safety, would prevent her from protecting Kevin and Rose Anne. When she pushed past him, he caught her by the shoulders at the far side of the bridge.

"Stay back!" shouted Leland.

"How did you find us?" Carolyn asked, her voice as placid as if her brother-in-law were a welcome visitor.

"I saw you at the urgent care clinic. Your boyfriend mentioned you lived in Evergreen Corners, so I decided to pay a call." His nose wrinkled. "Lousy place. Half the town is gone, and the rest of it stinks."

Michael couldn't hold back another groan. *He* had been the one to give Leland the way to burst back into her family's lives.

"Don't," she whispered. "Don't listen to him. He twists everything in the hope it'll hurt everyone more."

He nodded, knowing her composure might become their sole weapon against the man who was trying to push Kevin into the car, too. The boy fought, but couldn't escape his *daed*'s greater strength.

"Then I saw that locket," Leland taunted. "Did your sister ever tell you what I did when I discovered she'd wasted my hard-earned money on it?"

"Yes."

The simple dignity of her answer amazed Michael, who'd thought he couldn't be more astonished by Carolyn's quiet courage. She faced this horrible man in terror, for her hands quivered, but she refused to let him daunt her.

"I wasn't sure if these were my kids because they weren't the right ages." Leland snickered a derisive laugh. "Then I realized you'd changed their ages as well as their names. My seven-year-old son, Devon, became your five-year-old son, Kevin, while Rosina lost a year on her age and became Rose Anne. I didn't think you were that devious, Cora."

Cora?

Michael flinched. Had Cora been her name before she came to Evergreen Corners? He remembered Kevin saying she used to have a different name.

Something in his face must have betrayed his thoughts, because Leland laughed. "Guess you didn't tell your boyfriend everything. Maybe you're not so different from me when it comes to toeing the line on the rules."

"Let them go," she pleaded as she stepped from beneath the overhang at the edge of the bridge. "Please,

Leland. I'm sure we can work out something so you can have time with them."

He sneered at her, then snarled at Kevin to behave. The boy ignored him as Leland laughed with contempt. "Supervised visits with some social worker looking down her nose at me if I speak to them? No way! They're my kids, and they're coming with me."

"We're not your kids!" Kevin swung his foot and hit Leland hard in the shin.

The attack shocked Leland enough that his grip on the boy loosened. Giving his *daed* a shove out of the way, Kevin broke free. He reached into the car for his sister. Leland threw the boy to the ground.

Michael didn't hesitate. All his plans to avoid someone else's drama and live a peaceful life had been *dumm*. More than *dumm*. They'd been selfish. God hadn't put him on Earth to go through the motions of living while he kept his existence on an even keel. His Heavenly Father had given him something important to learn, and Michael had spent his life trying to avoid any situation where he might have to face that lesson.

No longer.

Stepping forward, he scooped Rose Anne out of the car. She tried to cling to him, but he put her next to her brother and ordered, "Kevin, go back to Carolyn."

The boy was scrambling to his feet. "But, Michael—"

"Go!" He kept his gaze locked with Leland's.

The other man seemed shocked by his overt defiance. So shocked he was frozen in indecision. Like other bullies, Leland didn't know how to react to someone standing up to him.

Rage twisted the man's face as he spat, "What do you think you're doing?"

Michael wished he could have prevented the *kinder* from hearing the curses spewing from their *daed*'s mouth. He didn't reply. Nothing he said would lessen the man's fury. At the same time, he intended to do all he could to keep Leland from taking the *kinder*.

A slim hand settled on his coat sleeve. "Let's go, Michael. We've got the children. There's nothing else for us here."

Leland pushed past Michael, raised his hand and drove it into Carolyn's face. She fell with a soft cry. The *kinder* screamed in horror as they knelt by where she sprawled on the dirt road.

Michael curled his own fingers into fists. How could he have been so stupid? He should have known Leland wouldn't attack a man his own size. Instead, he'd turned on Carolyn. As he took a step toward Leland, he heard her soft voice.

"Don't, Michael. It's not our way."

Our way? She'd walked away from her Amish life four years ago, taking the *kinder* with her and cutting them off from their faith and their heritage.

That was true, but she'd made what must have been a terrible choice in order to protect her nephew and niece from the man he faced, a man who'd struck her in a fit of fury that he hadn't been willing to expend on someone who might fight back.

Our way...

Her simple words proved she'd never set aside the life she'd loved, the life she would have given the *kinder* if she hadn't been trying to protect them from the one person who never should have been a threat to them.

Looking from her cheek that was already an angry red to his fists, he heard her voice echo in his mind. *Our way.*

A life of nonviolence was their way. Both his and Carolyn's. He couldn't set that aside. He'd prayed for more than a year for God to lead him in the direction he should go. It was with Carolyn and her *kinder*. It was among the Amish. It was a life of seeking peace.

He watched Leland make a fist again. Had his face revealed his thoughts? If so, there was nothing he would do to change what was going to happen. He steeled himself for the blow.

Carolyn cried out in horror as Michael wobbled and almost dropped to his knees when Leland hammered his fist into Michael's face. Blood exploded from his upper lip and his nose. Had Leland broken it?

God, forgive me for bringing him into this mess. Help us find a way out before the children are hurt, too.

Kevin stepped forward, but she pulled him back as she saw the triumphant smile Leland wore.

What could have been better for a bully who took delight in others' pain than to fight a man who wouldn't strike back?

Turn the other cheek to the evil-doer.

Michael was doing that, but she couldn't let him bear the brunt of Leland's cruelty.

"Kevin, Rose Anne, stay here," she ordered as her brother-in-law began to curl his hands into fists again.

If the *kinder* protested, she didn't hear them. Her heart was beating louder than thunder as she rushed forward. Thunder? In the winter on a cloudless night? The sound must be inside her battered skull.

She stepped between the men. "You aren't taking the *kinder*, Leland," she said as she confronted the brute with every bit of dignity she had in her.

"No? Who's going to stop me? You and your buddy, who doesn't seem good for much but being a punching bag?"

"You aren't taking the *kinder*."

Michael's hands clasped her shoulders, but she yanked them off, moving forward another step. He couldn't, with the best intentions aimed at keeping her safe, prevent her from protecting Kevin and Rose Anne.

"I'm done with running away," she said. "I'm done with hiding. I'm done with not being able to live a truthful life with God, but I'm not done with making sure these *kinder* are safe."

"Big words. You want to hear what I have to say? I'm done wasting time on you. Those kids are mine!" He drew back his arm.

She closed her eyes, trying to brace herself for another concussive blow.

It didn't come.

Feeling small arms encircling her legs, Carolyn opened her eyes to an astounding sight. Leland's arms were being held by Benjamin and Isaac and a couple of other men she couldn't identify in the clump of bodies.

Suddenly Leland popped out from among them. He dove into the car, started it and sent it skidding away from the bridge.

She heard sirens and realized the police had arrived. They were sent in pursuit of Leland's car, their tires squealing like a wounded animal.

Their rescuers came rushing to ask if they were okay. She didn't answer them as she threw her arms around the *kinder*, then reached out to Michael to draw him into their small circle. As he held them to his broad chest, she began to cry for all that had been lost and found in the past four years.

Chapter Sixteen

As soon as the trailer door was opened, Kevin and Rose Anne led Michael and Carolyn inside. Michael longed to close his eyes and lean back against the cushions and shut out the world until it stopped spinning like a maddened top. His head ached, and he couldn't see past the swelling around his left eye. Breathing made him sound like a beached trout, because he had to gasp for air through his mouth. His nose might not be broken, but it sure felt that way.

He was grateful they hadn't had to maneuver back across the weakened boards of the covered bridge. Her neighbors had assisted the *kinder*, Carolyn and him to where someone had built a wooden footbridge across the brook. He wondered how he'd missed that way across the brook earlier.

Everyone else stayed outside the cramped trailer. He heard someone offer to go for a *doktor* and someone else suggested opening the kitchen at the community center because it might be a long night while they waited to hear if Leland had been apprehended.

He sat on the narrow sofa while Rose Anne ran to the

bathroom. Her brother followed her, standing outside the closed door in a clear message that he didn't intend to let anyone threaten his sister again.

"Are you okay, Michael?" Carolyn whispered.

"I will be once Leland is caught."

"They'll catch him." She looked toward where Kevin now sat on her bed where he could keep an eye on the bathroom door.

He wished he shared her optimism. The authorities were on Leland's trail, and if he was nabbed, he'd be arrested. But only if they caught him.

"I'm sorry you got drawn into this." Her slow, careful motions warned she was hurting worse than she'd admit to.

Glen walked into the trailer without knocking. He gave them a grim nod, but motioned for them to stay where they were.

Michael realized the project director had taken on the same job Kevin had, guarding a door. People kept coming to the trailer, asking questions and trying to sort truth from the rumors raging through the village. Some of the tales were *dumm*, like the one that suggested the *kinder* had encountered a bear and were either dead or maimed.

Ja, they'd confronted a beast, but a human one.

He was relieved Glen was handling the door. Every time Michael spoke, his lip started bleeding again. He watched when Carolyn went to comfort Kevin, who was shaking so hard he feared the boy's slight body would come apart.

A rush of anger swelled as fast as his lip. What they'd witnessed tonight no *kind* should have to see and hear. If Leland had been thinking of anyone but himself, he would have realized he risked scarring his *kinder* for the rest of their lives. The thought of Kevin and Rose Anne being in their *daed*'s control sent a shudder of disgust through him.

"Michael?" asked Carolyn as she walked back to him.

Knowing she'd sensed his increased tension, he reached for her hand. He winced when he moved his thumb.

"I'm okay," he said past his split lip. "Confused my hand with a nail earlier today."

"Remind me not to let you teach Kevin how to use a hammer."

His smile became more sincere. She was doing what she always did. She was trying to make those around her feel better, though her own heart must have been hurting.

As soon as the bathroom door opened, Kevin jumped from the bed and threw his arms around his sister, startling her. Rose Anne began to cry. The poor *kind* had feared a man who was a stranger to her would take her away from the only *mamm* she knew.

Carolyn reached into the raised bed where Kevin slept. She pulled down the well-loved stuffed toys the *kinder* kept close each night.

"Here are some friends who want to see you," she murmured, her voice distorted by her bruised cheek, as she handed the dog and rabbit to the *kinder*.

Both Kevin and Rose Anne tossed the toys aside and threw their arms around her, clinging to her. Michael heard a sob slip through her lips, a sound she hadn't made even when she was knocked off her feet.

But he realized as he watched her put her arms around the *kinder*, her reaction was one of joy.

"I'm sorry," Kevin moaned.

"For what, dearest?" she asked.

"I was wrong," he said. "I like my name. I don't want the name that bad man gave me."

She knelt by the *kinder*. Though he knew how painful it must have been, she smiled. "He didn't give you those names. Your *mamm* did." She brushed the tearstains from their cheeks. "Devon, the name she gave you, Kevin, means divine because you are a gift from God. She chose Rosina as your name, Rose Anne, because it was the name of her favorite flower—a rose—and Ina, our mother's name, two things she cherished almost as much as she did you."

"Really?" asked Rose Anne.

"Really. You can choose if you want to be Kevin or Devon, Rose Anne or Rosina."

The two *kinder* looked at each other, overwhelmed. Carolyn must have seen that, too, because she stood, kissed them both on the head and said that no decision had to be made until they were ready.

The trailer door opened, and Glen stepped aside as Beth Ann walked up the steps. The midwife's eyes grew big as she stared at him and Carolyn, but she quickly recovered.

She had the *kinder* sit at the table and served them some orange juice she found in the refrigerator. From the tiny freezer, she pulled a tray of ice cubes. She put them in a bowl and frowned.

"Glen, have someone go over to the store and get some ice out of the box there." She didn't wait to see if he followed her order while she wrapped a handful of cubes in a dish towel. Handing it to Michael, Beth Ann said, "You will be using this for twenty minutes. I'll set the timer on the stove. When it beeps, take the ice off and let your skin rest for twenty minutes. Then keep repeating at least until the bleeding stops. Better yet, until the swelling starts to go down."

"All right." He was more than happy to spend the next twenty minutes sitting beside Carolyn, who was given a similar bundle of ice.

"Don't let the ice press directly against your skin," the midwife cautioned. "You don't want to cause more damage. Look at me, Michael."

He did, and she aimed a flashlight at each of his eyes before doing the same to Carolyn.

"Any double vision?" Beth Ann asked.

"No," they answered as one.

He smiled at Carolyn, who smiled back...and they both winced at the same time. But for the first time in a long time, he felt something he'd almost forgotten.

Happy.

When the children didn't protest going to sleep in her bed, Carolyn was astonished. Beth Ann had given Michael and her a cursory examination after they'd used the ice for tweny minutes and had said there were no signs of physical trauma, other than the skinned knee Kevin got when Leland shoved him away. Last Christmas Eve, the two had been too excited to sleep as they waited to unwrap the presents she'd bought for them as well as the ones she'd made.

This year, their gifts had been washed away in the October flood. The void in her heart that opened each time she'd thought of what they'd lost usually sent an ache deep within her. Tonight, she was celebrating she hadn't lost what was most precious to her.

"You need to use this again," Michael said, handing her an ice pack.

"It's been twenty minutes already?" She hadn't realized how long she'd been standing by the door, watching the children drift into their dreams and praying the nightmare they'd endured wouldn't follow them into their sleep.

"Ja." He took her hand and drew her back to sit beside him on the sofa.

She longed to lean her head on his broad shoulder, but brushing her aching cheek against his shirt sent a bolt of pain through her. She contented herself with sitting close enough to him that she could feel each shallow breath he took. Wondering how long it would be before he was able to breathe normally again, she hoped the doctor would arrive soon.

A soft knock came at the door. Was that the doctor at last? No, because Benjamin came in with Pastor Hershey on his heels. Without speaking, they motioned for Carolyn and Michael to remain where they were.

Only after the two men had joined Glen at the tiny table did Pastor Hershey ask, "Where are the children?"

"Asleep in the bedroom." She pointed toward the door that was slightly ajar.

"Can you make sure they're asleep?" Glen asked.

She started to nod, but halted as pain streaked through her head like a bolt of lightning. She pushed herself to her feet. When Michael stood, cupping her elbow, she whispered her thanks. Assuring herself the children were sound asleep, she walked back to the sofa.

Pastor Hershey spoke into the silence. "I've been informed Leland Reber is in custody."

"They caught him!" She breathed a sigh of relief.

"Not exactly."

"I don't understand."

Benjamin said quietly, "Leland either drove his car off the road or lost control of it. Whatever happened— and the police will determine that—he was discovered in the car, injured. He's on his way to the hospital now."

She started to put her hand to her lips. She caught herself before she could touch her aching face.

"He's going to be charged with assault and battery as well as abduction of a child. The last is the big felony. If convicted, he'll go to jail for a long time." The minister wore a grim smile. "Long enough for the children to grow up."

"Will they have to testify at the trial?" she asked.

"Let's deal with each problem as it comes," Pastor Hershey said, "and trust God to watch over His children, both big and small." He invited them to join him in prayer, and new tears fell down her cheeks when he included Leland in his supplications.

"Thank you," she said when he was finished.

"Of course." He stood.

Glen did, as well. "Let's get a good night's sleep tonight and tomorrow night before we head back to work the day after tomorrow. Installing drywall is nobody's favorite job. We'll start bright and early on Thursday on your walls, Carolyn."

"You're going to finish my house?"

Glen exchanged a bewildered frown with Benjamin before he looked at Michael as if hoping he'd explain what she meant. "Why wouldn't we finish your house, Carolyn?"

"I wasn't honest about who I am. I'm not a single mother, and I'm not Carolyn Wiebe. I'm Cora Hilty."

Glen put a calming hand on her shoulder. "You never told me or anyone here a lie. You *are* responsible for these two children, and you *are* in need of a home for them. What you call yourself isn't important. Nothing else matters to me or the organization I represent." He turned to Michael. "I assume the same could be said for Amish Helping Hands."

"I don't speak for the organization," he replied, "but I can't imagine any of us walking away before the house is finished. Especially me because I haven't had a chance to do that finishing work I've been looking forward to tackling."

Shortly after, with wishes for a Merry Christmas, the three men left, and for the first time that evening, it was quiet in the trailer.

Michael took her hand. When she looked at him, suddenly shy when she thought of everything they'd left in limbo, he said, "It's over, Carolyn."

"Cora," she replied. What would her real name sound like on his lips?

She almost laughed at how his split lip distorted every word he spoke, but the laughter would have been laced with tears. After four years of fearing Leland Reber was ready to ambush her and the *kinder*, tonight she didn't have to pray another day would come and go without his finding them.

"You're going to need to decide what you want to do now, Carolyn." He grinned. "I mean, Cora. It's going to take me some time to get used to your new-old name."

"Me, too."

"What do you plan to do?"

"First I have to forgive Leland."

"Can you?"

"I must." She closed her eyes, but opened them again when anguish swelled through her head. "Something is wrong in his heart. I saw it just after he struck me. He was terrified you would hurt him. I don't know when or how or who, but someone, sometime, somewhere hurt him, and it did something to his heart. I will pray he finds healing in God's love."

Michael regarded her without speaking, then leaned forward and pressed his lips to her forehead. "Will you be able to forgive yourself, too, when you did the only thing you could to safeguard the *kinder*?"

"I'm going to try. I'm going to write my friends in Indiana and let them know where we are."

"I'm sure they'll want you to come there."

"Most likely."

"I see."

She hesitated when she heard all the emotion vanish from his voice like water down a drain. Tossing aside all caution, she asked, "What do you see?"

"What do you mean?"

"Are you going to sit there and tell me you don't care if Kevin, Rose Anne and I go back to Indiana while you return to your life in New York?"

His eyes snapped as they had on the bridge. "Of course I care. But I won't let my yearnings get in the way of what you think is best for the *kinder*."

"What's best for them is to be with someone who loves them as much as I do." She put her hand on his uninjured cheek. "And that's you. Kevin has adored you since you met, and Rose Anne, like always, wasn't far behind him. However, this time, I wasn't, either. I want you in our lives, Michael."

"Are you asking me to marry you, Cora Hilty? Proposing to a man isn't something a plain woman would do."

"You need to know that I intend to live an Amish life...starting tomorrow."

"So you can propose to me tonight?" His eyes twinkled with merriment. "Well, you're too late."

"What?" She sat straighter, then wished she hadn't when pain arced across her head. "What do you mean I'm too late? Have you made up your mind about baptism?"

"*Ja*, I've decided. But Kevin already asked me to marry you and become his *daed-onkel*."

"He did?"

"When he mentioned you were his *mamm-aenti*." Leaning his forehead against hers, he said, "I never gave him an answer, and then I was a complete fool when you told me about Leland." He told her what he'd decided on the bridge when he faced Leland and made his choice of the life he wanted. "God opened my heart to Him and showed me that my life should be lived as an Amish man."

"I'm so happy for you, Michael."

"And be happy for yourself, because my answer to Kevin's proposal and yours is *ja*. I want to marry you, even if I can't remember what to call you right now. Why don't I call you my future wife?"

"*Ich liebe dich*, Michael Miller." She kissed him on his cheek.

He traced a feathery line along her lips. "As soon as I can, I want a real kiss."

"As many as you want, especially if it takes the rest of my life to give them all to you."

Epilogue

"And here are the keys to your new home," Pastor Hershey said after blessing the completed house.

Applause exploded through the cold, crisp day. Cameras clicked as many of the witnesses, who'd also participated in rebuilding the charming house that overlooked Washboard Brook, raised their phones to record the family taking possession of their new home. Two dozen red, white and blue balloons rose into the sky.

Mr. and Mrs. Gagnon, both leaning on walkers, smiled before taking the keys and opening the door to the second house finished by the volunteers in Evergreen Corners. Cheers rose through the cold afternoon, and the nattily dressed anchors from the local TV stations followed the elderly couple into the house.

Standing in the shadows of the trees separating her new home from the Gagnons', Cora clapped. The joy on the Gagnons' faces was a testament to the hard work and the faith of the community in coming together to rebuild. Glen's grin had barely fit onto his face as he accepted congratulations from several state government officials and spoke to a reporter from the high school newspaper.

Michael crossed the snow-covered yard that would be planted with sod in the spring. Unlike her, he bore a scar from the encounter with Leland. It was a small half circle near where he'd been struck in the mouth. She thought it made him look rather rakish.

Beside him, Kevin and Rosina were sharing a box of popcorn. She smiled as she watched them acting like normal *kinder* as they giggled at something Michael had said before running off to see their friends.

Kevin had insisted on keeping the name she'd given him, but his little sister changed her name back to the one given to her by her *mamm* in honor of the *grossmammi* she'd never known. Remembering Rosina's name was becoming easier, and everyone in town seemed comfortable changing from Carolyn to Cora. There were slipups, but they all laughed them off.

"It could have been your celebration," Michael said when he reached her. They walked back through the woods toward the charming little house where she and the *kinder* lived. "Now that Leland is in jail, you don't have to worry about him seeing you and the *kinder* on TV or in the newspapers."

"I didn't need a celebration." She smiled as she laced her fingers through his when they climbed up the steps to the inviting front porch where she planned to put rocking chairs once the weather warmed. "How can I expect Kevin and Rosina to embrace their plain heritage if I step in front of a camera?"

"They seem happy with learning to be Amish."

"Except for complaining about having to sit still during church services."

He laughed. "As Gabriel and I did when we were kids."

"Regina and I did, too." She smiled at the memory that was no longer tainted by one man's cruelty.

"Do you want to join the party next door? I don't want you to miss this one when you missed having one of your own."

"You volunteers came to the house when it was blessed and Glen gave me the keys. Besides, it doesn't seem right to have a celebration when we won't be living here for long."

"For at least six months. It'll take that long before we can have our wedding."

She smiled. "I'm glad you could come here today for the celebration."

As planned, Michael had returned to Harmony Creek Hollow on New Year's Day and had been helping his brother prepare for planting. He'd also been taking classes so he could be baptized in the spring. When he could, he caught a ride in one of the *Englisch* vans to Evergreen Corners bringing volunteers for a short stint.

He grinned. "I didn't come for the celebration. I've got lots of kisses to collect, as you recall."

She didn't have a chance to say she was ready when he was because Gladys Whittaker walked into the yard. "May I speak with you, Michael?"

He arched his brows at Cora, then went down the steps.

Wondering why the mayor wanted to speak to Michael, Cora went into the house that already felt like home. She took off her boots and hung up her coat and bonnet on the pegs by the door. Touching the Amish *kapp* she wore once again, she looked around her. The stone counters glistened like the wood floors beneath the rag rugs she'd made. The living room was partially furnished, but thanks to her work for the diner and other orders for baked goods, she'd been able to buy a sofa where she cuddled with the *kinder* at day's end. She was home schooling them, focusing on the topics they'd study in a plain school. After three months, Kevin and Rosina were doing lessons at their true grade levels.

As it did every time she came into the house, her gaze went to a small shelf on the living room wall between the two windows that offered a view of the brook. The house's sole decoration, other than a calendar hanging in the kitchen, was set on the shelf. The small sculpture of a hawk with its wings spread wide to capture a thermal sat there. It wasn't the same pose as the statue that had been swallowed by the flood.

When Michael had brought it to her and explained how Kevin had spoken of the wooden hawk, she'd been awed by Michael's artistic skill. She'd seen only the rough birds and boats he'd taught her nephew to whittle. The hawk, which was less than six inches high, looked so real she half expected it to rise up off her palm and soar into the sky.

Pounding his feet, Michael came into the house and took off his boots. He set them beside hers. Knowing this man would put his boots next to hers for the rest of their lives sent happiness pulsing through her.

Before she could ask what the mayor had told him, he asked, "Are you sure you want to leave Evergreen Corners?"

"No, but there's no Amish community here."

"What if someone started one?"

She looked at him in astonishment. "Are you saying you're willing to stay?"

"Why not? You've got six acres here. Not enough for a

farm, but enough for a family garden and a chicken coop and a shop for me to work in while I'm building new library shelves for the ones ruined in the flood as well as supervising the repairs on the first floor of the town hall."

"What?"

His eyes were bright with happiness. "Gladys offered me enough work to keep me busy for a year or more. By the time I'm done with work for the village, I should be able to find other jobs to keep me busy."

"But what about your baptism classes?"

"We can travel to Harmony Creek Hollow every other weekend. It's about time you and the *kinder* met my brother and his wife and their *kinder*. I can take baptism classes on Saturdays, and then we can attend the services on Sunday. It will give Kevin and Rosina a chance to see what it's like to live in a plain settlement. What do you think?"

She grasped his hands as she stood face-to-face with him. "I think you're *wunderbaar*, Michael Miller."

He chuckled as he did whenever she spoke in *Deitsch*. "You're pretty special yourself, Cora Hilty, and I think I need to start collecting my kisses starting now."

His lips brushed her cheek, and she closed her eyes as delight danced through her. His broad fingers curved on her shoulders as his mouth found hers. His kiss was as gentle as a spring breeze luring a leaf to unfurl, and she softened against him. After so many dark years, he'd brought joy into her life and she could not wait to spend every day and night together for the rest of their lives.

He raised his head when noise came from the front porch.

"Sounds like the *kinder* got tired of playing in the

snow," she whispered, running her fingertips along his strong jaw.

"So I hear." He kissed the tip of her nose. "Well, in that case, I'd better get to work."

"You're starting on the library shelves *now*?"

"I need to work on your house. On *our* house." He leaned toward her and whispered, "I don't know how the other volunteers are going to feel about me pulling out their wiring to make it a real Amish house."

"We'll break it to them when they're in a *gut* mood."

"And when will that be?"

"When they come to our wedding celebration."

"You have the best ideas, *liebling*." He laughed again. "Or as Rosina would say, the *gut-est*."

* * * * *

If you enjoyed this story,
don't miss these other books
from Jo Ann Brown:

The Amish Suitor
The Amish Christmas Cowboy
The Amish Bachelor's Baby
The Amish Widower's Twins

Find more great reads at www.LoveInspired.com.

Dear Reader,

Sometimes, the worst events bring out the best in people. We met many of our new neighbors when a hurricane swept through our town, and we were outside cleaning debris. Those who were able stepped up without fanfare to help those who weren't, and within a week, our neighborhood looked just as it should have. But we had a new camaraderie that lasted far longer than the scars of damage.

The Mennonite Disaster Service was established seventy years ago when a group of young people wanted to help others. MDS volunteers, who are both plain and *Englisch*, come primarily from the US and Canada and have helped rebuild homes and lives after disasters, usually weather related or due to wildfires.

Visit me at www.joannbrownbooks.com. Look for my next book, again set in Evergreen Corners, Vermont, coming soon.

Wishing you many blessings,
Jo Ann Brown

WE HOPE YOU ENJOYED THIS BOOK!

New beginnings. Happy endings. Discover uplifting inspirational romance.

Look for six new Love Inspired books available every month, wherever books are sold!

LIHALO2019

SPECIAL EXCERPT FROM

"You won't have to stay on our account, and we can look after Ernest's place, too. I can hire a man to help me. Someone I know I can…" Ruth's words trailed away.

Trust? Depend on? Was that what Ruth was going to say? She didn't want him around. She couldn't have made it any clearer. Maybe it had been a mistake to think he could patch things up between them, but he wasn't willing to give up after only one day. Ruth was nothing if not stubborn, but he could be stubborn, too.

Owen leaned back and chuckled.

"What's so funny?"

"I'm here until Ernest returns, Ruth. You can't get rid of me with a few well-placed insults."

She huffed and turned her back to him. "I didn't insult you."

"Ah, but you wanted to. I'd like to talk about my plans in the morning."

Ruth nodded. "You know my feelings, but I agree we both need to sleep on it."

Owen picked up his coat and hat, and left for his uncle's farm. The wind was blowing harder and the snow was piling up in growing drifts. It wasn't a fit night out for man nor beast. As if to prove his point, he found Meeka, Ernest's big guard dog, lying across the corner of the porch out of the wind. Instead of coming out to greet him, she whined repeatedly.

He opened the door of the house. "Come in for a bit." She didn't get up. Something was wrong. Was she hurt? He walked toward her. She sat up and growled low in her throat. She had never done that to him before. "Are you sick, girl?"

She looked back at something in the corner and whined softly. Over the wind he heard what sounded like a sobbing child. "What have you got there, Meeka? Let me see."

He came closer. There was a child in an Amish bonnet and bulky winter coat trying to bury herself beneath Meeka's thick fur. Where had she come from? Why was she here? He looked around. Where were her parents?

Don't miss
The Hope *by Patricia Davids,*
available now wherever
HQN™ books and ebooks are sold.

HQNBooks.com